The Secret
of the Northern Lights

The Secret
of the Northern Lights

W.P. Kinsella

THISTLEDOWN PRESS LTD.

Canadian Cataloguing in Publication Data
Kinsella, W. P.
The secret of the northern lights
ISBN 1-895449-85-5
I. Title.
PS8571.I57 S42 1998   C813'.54   C98-920056-6
PR9199.3.K443 S42 1998

Book and cover design by J. Forrie
Typeset by Thistledown Press Ltd.
Cover painting by J. Forrie

Printed and bound in Canada by
Veilleux Impression à Demande
. Boucherville, Quebec

Thistledown Press Ltd.
633 Main Street
Saskatoon, Saskatchewan
S7H 0J8

**Saskatchewan
Arts Board**

THE CANADA COUNCIL | LE CONSEIL DES ARTS
FOR THE ARTS | DU CANADA
SINCE 1957 | DEPUIS 1957

Thistledown Press gratefully acknowledges the financial assistance of
the Canada Council for the Arts, the Saskatchewan Arts Board, and the
Government of Canada through the Book Publishing Industry
Development Program for its publishing program.

Contents

For Lee and Maggie Harwood

Bleaching the Buffalo

Whew!" says my friend Frank Fencepost, "that waitress must have sprayed on her perfume with a crop duster."

I have to agree. We just come out of a restaurant on the Interstate in North Dakota, not too far from where we heading with our precious cargo. That perfume was thick as hair spray in the air, make us both cough and clear our throats.

The precious cargo is riding in an air-conditioned animal trailer attached to the GMC King Cab that pulling it. Me and Frank been hired to drive right through, eighteen hours straight, to Fargo, North Dakota. We don't have a key to the animal trailer, there ain't even a window for us to peek inside.

"There's a three-day supply of food and water available inside in there. Everything's computerized, monitored both from here and Fargo. There's a speed control on the truck won't allow you to travel more than 55 mph. If one of you guys drives while the other rests, allowing for gas and food stops you'll arrive in Fargo in eighteen hours and fifty minutes. You'll be paid in cash when you get there with the cargo safe and sound. Any questions?"

"Yeah," says Frank. "How come we drive on a parkway and park in a driveway?"

"What's that got to do with anything?" says the guy who hired us. His name is Mr. Stevenson and he wear a very expensive western suit, a huge white Stetson, and snakeskin cowboy boots, got pointy silver toe caps that glitter like diamonds.

"You said you was takin' questions," says Frank.

"I meant about your job."

"My job is ministering to the spiritually destitute. I am a philosopher, and creator of Brother Frank's Gospel Hour, a radio program, TV show, and traveling Evangelical Crusade. Me and my friend here, Three Big Bunions, a fellow I salvaged from skid row, ain't that right BB? is just taking a little holiday."

Though we been hanging around for a few days this is the first time we met Mr. Stevenson.

"It's invigorating for me to get in touch with the common people every so often," Frank go on. "I could ask you some questions about my job but I doubt you'd be able to answer them."

"I meant this job that you've been hired for," yell Mr. Stevenson. Mr. S. is one of the owners, and in charge of shipping this here half-growed white buffalo to Fargo, where it going to be displayed in a bulletproof glass pen at a rodeo and pow-wow.

Me and Frank and our friends are on the road about half of every year. Frank preach his message of What would it take to make you happy? to arenas full of people, while we pass the collection plates and stay up late in the night counting the money. Bedelia Coyote keep her hand on the pulse of the whole operation, audit the money, see that Frank really do put a good percentage back into helping people make their dreams come true. She pay each of us a salary, plus I write a newspaper column that get sent to five hundred or so papers, where I print letters from people in need, dispense money if their cause is good, like a grandma want to visit a new grandchild, somebody need to pay their heating bill, or a person need new glasses they can't get no other way.

I always dreamed of having all the money I ever needed, and so did Frank. What we find now that we got money is that life ain't all that different. Instead of traveling in Louis Coyote's pickup truck, we travel in an old bus, and later on a new one with air conditioning. Instead of staying in hotels where the washroom was down the hall and they charge a five dollar deposit on the key, we stay at hotels where a guy in a uniform carries your suitcase for you. We order room service any time we feel like it, and we can afford to pay the bill instead of skipping down the fire escape. We also don't have to play gas-and-run when we fill up the bus at a service station.

Frank read more than one newspaper every day, look for preaching ideas. A year or more ago he seen an item about a white buffalo calf being born on a farm in Michigan or Minnesota or one of them "M" states.

"Silas, make sure that next year Bedelia schedule Brother Frank's Gospel Hour to appear somewhere close to where this buffalo live," and Frank rip the article out of *USA Today*, even though the paper belong to the restaurant where we eating breakfast.

Frank and me understand that a white buffalo is significant to Native American Mythology, though we're not certain of the details. One native leader is quoted in *USA Today* as saying the white buffalo is about the same importance to Indians as the second coming would be to Christians.

"We got to pay that buffalo a visit," says Frank. "Soon as possible. I'll get some inspiration for my preaching, and you'll get an idea or two for stories. I'll nose around to make certain they earning all the money they ought to off this buffalo. Maybe I can sell my business expertise to the owners."

"It's good to see you're your usual modest self," I say. "I'd hate to see success go to your head."

A few days ago we finish up a tour in Wisconsin, which border on a couple of these "M" states. Our friends head back to Alberta on the bus. Me and Frank rent a car and drive off to see the buffalo, which is on display at a corporate farm where we have to pay ten dollars each in order to get inspiration from it.

What can I say? The buffalo is about half growed, look like any other buffalo I ever seen except it is white as a snowbank, have bluish eyes, and its hair look like it been treated at a beauty salon. We find out later it has been beautified by an animal hairstylist. I would never have suspected such people exist. There are actually shampoos and conditioners for horses and dogs and monkeys, and probably hamsters. This is really odd to guys like me and Frank who, until we were about eighteen, washed our own hair in the slough downhill from Blue Quills hall, with a bar of Ivory soap that float like a bob on a fish line. Use a worn out shirt and sunshine to dry with.

We arrive for our look at the buffalo just as they getting him ready to make a major trip.

"He's going to be on display at a big rodeo and pow-wow in North Dakota," say the man who collect ten dollars from each of us. By being at the pow-wow it will give thousands of Native Americans the opportunity to see this sacred buffalo.

"You're all heart," says Frank. "I can see where this is a community service, have nothing to do with the ten dollars you collect from each of those Native Americans."

"Actually, the entrance fee will be fifteen dollars in North Dakota."

"That's what I'd charge," says Frank, smile big. "How do you figure I could get in on the act?" He go on to explain about Brother Frank's Gospel Hour.

"I got one bit of advice for you, son," that fellow say. "Get your own white buffalo." Turn out this corporation that own the buffalo bought it from another corporation who bought it from an entrepreneur, who bought it from somebody else who may or may not have been the original owner.

"Right. I knew that," says Frank. But we hang around, get to know everybody, eventually get trusted enough that they hire us to drive the truck with the sacred buffalo in it to North Dakota.

"If we can't trust a preacher, who can we trust?" say one of the foreman.

I could answer that but I don't.

The trailer is really fancy. Actually, there are two trailers. Ever since he was a baby the white buffalo have a friend live with him, someone to keep him from being lonely and to kick his heels up with. A plain little brown buffalo.

"Brownie there has served his purpose," says that same foreman. "We can't afford to ship him around the country, and Whitey (as the white buffalo been imaginatively named) will be traveling most of his life from now on, and better get used to doing it alone."

"Where's the other buffalo off to?" I ask. I figure a park or zoo.

"He's heading for that great buffalo jump in the sky."

"How come?"

"You ever hear of buffalo burgers, buffalo steak, roast buffalo? Well, that meat don't come from chickens."

The trailers are exactly alike.

"How do you know which one's which?" ask Frank.

"Don't be ridiculous," says the foreman. "The trailers don't matter. If there's one thing we know it's how to tell a white buffalo from a regular one.

It seem to me that there may be something more going on here than meet the eye. What we're doing remind me of a book I read about the break in at Watergate, only we're more organized. We're expected to take off at 3:00 AM. We even have to synchronize our watches with the guys in charge, and with the fellows who going to drive the other buffalo to the stockyards. I wear a Timex with a picture of Kim Campbell, the lady who was Prime Minister of Canada for about two weeks. Chief Tom Crow-eye, who is in the Alberta Government, hand them out to impress us. Ms. Campbell lose the election anyway. Frank, soon as he have some money, buy a watch have so many dials it look like the cockpit of an air plane.

"Roger, good buddy," Frank says, "this here watch is so smart it got a university degree in Time Management. The relative humidity is 29%, it's seven miles to the nearest Nudie bar, and my birthday falls on a Wednesday this year."

"Just make sure you're on time," says the foreman.

We wheel the trailer out on the Interstate, right behind the other trailer, driven by a big, blond guy with a beer belly and a brush cut, which wheel off to a ramp gonna take him and his buffalo to the stockyards.

At 4:00 AM it ain't so difficult to tell you being followed. Behind us is a black pickup truck with three people in it.

When we go as fast as the speed control allow they stay behind us, when we slow down to 35 mph they still stay behind us.

When we stop for coffee, they stop, too. I eye them pretty careful when they take a booth across and ahead of us. There are two short, squat Indians in denim rodeo gear, and hats that been out on the range in bad weather. The third guy is unforgettable. He is tall with tight, tobacco-colored skin stretched over high cheekbones. He's wearing a black hat with a band of silver conches around the crown, on his neck and hands are about a pound of turquoise and silver jewelry. When he glance at us I feel like he bored a couple of holes in me; he has coyote-yellow eyes that glint like moonlight on chrome.

"I think those guys are following us," I say to Frank, who turn and take a long look at them.

Frank is usually subtle as a rock slide or flash flood, and this time is no exception. He stand up, stretch himself, walk down the aisle to their table.

"I seen you looking at us," Frank says. The three of them sit silent staring straight ahead. "I figure it's because you can't quite place me. Being a celebrity I'm used to having that happen to me. My name is J. Frank Fencepost. You've probably seen me on TV or listen to me on the radio, maybe you even drop by one of our crusades: Brother Frank's Gospel Hour, the place where dreams come true."

Frank is running out of steam. He might as well be invisible for all the attention they paying to him.

"I'm Brother Frank. Usually I charge $7.50 for autographs, money go for a good cause. But for fans like you I'll make an exception and sign for free. Just hand me your napkins there . . . "

"We weren't looking at you," the tall, handsome one say.

"Just like you weren't following us? We may not have been born yesterday, but we act like we were."

Frank leave them to figure on that for a minute. The two stocky guys start to rise up from their seats. Oh, boy, that means I'm gonna have to help Frank fight whether I want to or not.

Just as the first guy come sliding out of the booth, a waitress appear with a plate of food in each hand, a platter of steak and eggs on her arm.

"You guys go ahead and eat," says Frank. "Don't let me interrupt you. Trust me, you'll feel better once you get your stomachs full. We'll talk later, eh? Nice to visit with you."

We leave money on the table for our coffee, plus a big tip, head right back onto the Interstate.

But a few miles down the road that truck turn up in our rearview again. They never leave us out of sight but they never make a move on us either, and the next time we stop to eat they're no where to be seen, but they pick us up again soon as we hit the Interstate.

We are an hour or two ahead of schedule when we get to Fargo. We pull into a service station, all the way around behind where we can't be found unless someone is looking for us.

Frank look at me and nod toward the trailer. We both know Frank has this special relationship with locks. He claim he can open some just by staring at them. For others he needs a paper clip, a nail, or a coat hanger.

"Something weird's going on," says Frank. "I think we should have a look at the buffalo."

For once I agree.

Frank barely have to shake the lock before it pop open. We pull open the door of the trailer. We are hit by nice, cool, air-conditioned air, smell pretty much like a buffalo been in there for close to two days. It take a few seconds for our eyes to accustom to the dimness, but as soon as we can see, we realize there is a serious problem.

"This buffalo ain't white," says Frank, stating the obvious.

"We'd better close this trailer up fast, deliver this buffalo and get across the border to Canada before they blame us for the mistake," I say.

"I agree," says Frank. "Though who do you think they gonna blame? Us? Or the foreman who mix up the buffaloes at the other end? And, what do you suppose happen to the real white buffalo?"

"I don't want to think about it. I just hope the stockyards take a close look at him before they turn him into hamburgers."

"What if they don't? What do you think of the idea of us delivering a white buffalo to Fargo, just like we was supposed to do."

"How can we do that?"

"One time I seen Connie Bigcharles turn her hair blond by using a couple of cans of spray-on stuff she got at the drug store. This here buffalo is a light brown, while Connie's hair was black as a crow wing."

"What if we took him to a beauty shop?" I say.

We go to a pay phone at the service station, call the number we been given in case of emergency.

"We got a flat tire," we tell them, "take about two hours to get it fixed. We don't mention we are early into Fargo, they now not expecting us for four hours.

We drive into downtown Fargo, a city that sit like a button on a plate, in the middle of the endless green prairie of North

Dakota. We stop at a drug store where Frank buy up about a gallon of hydrogen peroxide, and a dozen bottle of products have *Sun* in their name, the kind that supposed to make your hair light like you been on a beach all summer, and some bottles of stuff you can brush into your hair make you beautiful and blond.

We park in an empty lot next to a vacant building, open the trailer and have a go at spraying the buffalo, who is in such a small space he ain't got much choice but to co-operate with us. The buffalo seem to be tame, is wearing a halter, and the walls of the stall inside the trailer cozy up to his sides so he can't move much.

"What we need is some Head and Shoulders Shampoo," says Frank. "This fellow's hair is a little greasy."

The buffalo have a fairly long mane and long hair down his front, while the rest of him that we can see is covered in soft, curly hair an inch or so long.

"Where do we start?" I say.

"At the beginning," says Frank, hold up a piece of mane, pour a more than ample amount of hydrogen peroxide, comb it in with Frank's personal comb that he use on his own braids.

The buffalo make a sad call, half moo, half cough. Guess the smell of the hydrogen peroxide don't agree with him any more than it does with us.

We splash, and brush, and comb, and spray. But not a lot change that we can see.

Frank reads the instructions on one of the bottles. "This one says we ought to expose him to bright sunlight in order for his hair to bleach. You figure if we was to back him out into the parking lot he could sun for a while?"

"How would we get him back in? He ain't full grown but he's big enough to go about anywhere he damn pleases."

We are thinking this over when that truck with the three cowboys drive by slow, go to the end of the block, turn around and drive our way again.

I notice there is a broom in the corner of the trailer. I use a trick I seen in a western movie once. I lean the broom in my arms like a gun, stand half-hidden between the trailer and the truck, let the broom stick out like a rifle barrel.

As the car full of cowboys slow down across the road, I let them see part of me and the gun barrel. They stare at us for a couple of minutes, then move on.

Behind the trailer, some parts of Frank and Frank's clothes are bleaching, but the buffalo look same as always. While I been scaring off the strange cowboys, Frank back the buffalo out, have his halter tied to the doorknob of the trailer, while he make good wishes about the buffalo lightening up because of the sunshine.

Nothing seem to work and time going by. I unhook the trailer from the truck, leave Frank, the broom, the trailer and the buffalo in the parking lot, and drive the truck out into an industrial district, find a one-block strip mall which is pretty old and have graffiti wrote on some of its walls.

I spot a place called Crystal's Beauty Salon next door to Pete's Cafe, and a Nothing Over a Dollar Store. It is 10:00 AM and Miss Crystal herself is just unlocking the door to her salon.

"Miss Crystal," I say. "I got about the strangest request you ever gonna hear. It's too long a story for me to explain why, but we need you to bleach a buffalo for us, make him platinum blond, and in a hurry. He's not full grown and he's friendlier than the average buffalo, but by noon today it is real important that he be white.

Miss Crystal look too young to own a beauty salon herself, she has beautiful upswept golden hair, big gold ringlets in front of her ears could pass for jewelery they so carefully done. She has friendly blue eyes and a smile that make me smile even though I'm pretty worried.

"That is a challenge," Miss Crystal say. Then she look at me and laugh. "Ain't life crazy?"

"We have the money to pay you cash," I assure her.

"That's peachy. What you want can be done. Though I've never beautified a whole animal body. I own horses, I do their manes and tails, shampoo, color, conditioner, make them look like society ladies. Where's your buffalo?"

"He's in a parking lot, over yonder about a dozen blocks." I point in the direction where I'd guess Frank and the buffalo are.

"You'll have to bring him to the shop."

"We'll give it a try."

"My assistant will be in in a few minutes and we've got a light morning." She smile at me again. "This is gonna be so much fun."

Back at the parking lot, Frank having a certain amount of difficulty. The buffalo have a definite mind of his own, set his heart on traveling backwards. He got the rope taut, his neck stretched out so we can see all his tendons, and he is inching the trailer across the lot.

"He don't aim to go back in the trailer," says Frank.

I tell Frank about Miss Crystal's Beauty Salon.

"We could drive the truck, let the truck pull the trailer, let the trailer pull the buffalo. Or, we could both of us take the halter rope and try to lead the buffalo ourselves."

We decide the two of us can lead him.

He is one frisky buffalo. He has a way of going sideways about as much as he goes forward. Also, for whatever reason, he like to walk on the sidewalk not on the street. Every time a truck rumble by, the buffalo pick up speed, even though both Frank's and my boots are making black stripes on the sidewalk, the kind air planes make when they touch down on a runway.

We are about half way to Miss Crystal's when a police car pull up alongside us.

"I bet there's probably a reason you're walking a buffalo down the street," says the cop, who is young and not likely acquainted with many buffalo.

"What kind of reason would you believe?" asks Frank.

"Try me."

"He ain't stolen," I say, which may not have been the best thing I could of said.

"We're bringing him into town for an appointment at the big rodeo and pow-wow next week. This here is Ferdinand, the world's only tap dancing buffalo. We're giving him his exercise and taking him to a beauty parlor, where he gonna get shampooed and curled, tied with red ribbons and sprayed with perfume. You want to see him do a couple of steps? If you was to whistle 'Home on the Range', he'd waltz right across the street with you."

"What beauty salon?" says the cop, figure he's caught us in a lie.

"Miss Crystal's Beauty Salon," I say, "next door to Pete's Cafe, by the Nothing Over a Dollar Store."

He look at us with narrowed eyes. "As long as you keep him on a leash and out of traffic, I can't see you're breaking any law. I'll drop by Crystal's in a few minutes to make sure you're telling the truth."

"He's the only buffalo in the world can polka," says Frank. "Used to appear with Weird Al Yankovic, before that Lawrence Welk. Bring your accordion to the beauty shop."

We are pretty sweated up by the time we get the buffalo into the parking lot behind Miss Crystal's.

"Life is strange," says Miss Crystal, as she step out the back door, wearing a pink smock, carrying a box of beauty supplies. "You know it would be a lot simpler if we could work indoors. I had some horse shampoo in my car, and I called the beauty supply wholesale to send over some extra jugs of lightener."

We've named the buffalo Chief Tom. We try to lead him into the shop, but no way will he step into the dark doorway.

"For goodness sakes," says Miss Crystal. "You boys never lived on a farm? I was raised on a cattle spread down Ashgrove way, south of Bismarck. Give me a minute here."

She disappear into the shop, come back with a big white towel, tie it carefully around Chief Tom's head to make a blindfold.

"He'll be gentle as a baby, now," she says. "Let me take that lead," and she take the rope from me and Frank, whisper in Chief Tom's ear, walk him into the beauty salon like he was a regular customer. "Ain't he the cutest thing," she says as she ties his lead to a chair with a fancy-looking knot.

I bet it would surprise you to know how much it cost to bleach a ½ sized buffalo. Miss Crystal make Frank show his roll of bills before she start the work. She shampoo Chief Tom's mane, combing in the bleach, then set about to bleach him, working on patches the size of a square foot each time.

"No way I can get finished by noon," she tells us. So we phone in again, claim that a rim broke and we'll be another hour late.

When it come time for Miss Crystal to bleach Chief Tom's face, and around his eyes and ears, that buffalo get a little frisky, start backing up with purpose, do a certain amount of damage to a wall, a mirror, a counter, one of them reclining salon chairs, and scare the wits out of her assistant, Mr. Bruce, and a couple of blue-haired ladies he's working on up at the front of the shop. Miss Crystal take a minute to add the damages to our bill.

I go pick up the trailer and the truck while Frank supervise the rest of the bleaching. I stop in at Pete's Cafe get us a take-out order of hamburgers and fries, and by the time I get back to the salon the job is done. Chief Tom, though he look a bit more platinum blond than the real white buffalo, would fool a lot of people, we hope.

"I believe a fifty dollar tip would be in order," Miss Crystal says. "My salon's going to smell like buffalo for years to come."

"I caught most of the problem in a plastic tub after he decide to relieve himself," says Frank.

"It's the word *most* that bothers me," says Miss Crystal, "and, oh yes, one plastic tub $14.95."

"We sure are grateful for what you done for us," says Frank. "I'll say a prayer for you on Brother Frank's Gospel Hour. You be sure to listen in."

"Jesus H.," says the guy who meet us at the rodeo grounds, after he open up the trailer and look at Chief Tom. "Jesus H.," he says again. "How did this happen?"

"How did what happen?" we say. We had intended to get away from there real quick in case someone recognized our buffalo as a fake, but they insisted on checking out the merchandise before they paid us. We need the wages because after Frank pay for bleaching the buffalo, the damages to the salon, plus a hundred dollar tip, our wallets are pretty empty.

"Beau? James Earl?" this fellow call to his friends, "come have a look at this."

Two men in expensive cowboy clothes appear.

They look.

"Jesus H.," the first guy says again.

"I don't see how they could have screwed up like this," says James Earl, who is about 6′ 5″ with a head the shape of a butcher's block.

We stand by shifting our feet and trying to act innocent.

"I guess it's safe to tell you now that you're here, that fact is . . . you two were supposed to be decoys. You were supposed to be transporting a second, regular little buffalo in here."

"The one that was going to the stockyards?"

"That's just what we let on was happening," says James Earl. "You were supposed to carry the brown buffalo, but think that you had the real thing. It was all done for security. Everyone was supposed to think you were carrying the real thing."

"See, there are some radical Indians who want the white buffalo for themselves," says Beau, who is squat and paunchy, with a Texas drawl that won't quit.

"They think it's a religious icon or something," says the Jesus H. guy, whose name near as I can make out is Stook. "We heard they might try to kidnap Whitey, so we sent you out as decoys. Whitey was supposed to be in that other trailer. He's supposed to arrive here tomorrow at noon."

"Did y'all have any trouble on the drive down?" ask Beau.

We tell them about the truck full of cowboys.

"Somebody's gonna lose their job over this," says Stook. "This here prize buffalo's been endangered and got here by pure luck, while some useless brown buffalo is riding around the country in air-conditioned comfort."

When they give us our pay there is a five hundred dollar cash bonus for each of us for scaring off the would-be kidnappers.

"Let's get out of North Dakota quick as we can," says Frank.

We take a taxi to the airport. While we waiting for a flight to Calgary, sitting in the cafeteria minding our own business, who should come along but the three kidnapper-cowboys. They march right up to us, their boots clicking on the cold floor. Their leader, the guy with coyote-yellow eyes, and one of the short guys sit down at our table without being asked. The third guy stands guard, I guess in case we decide to run somewheres.

"We need to talk," the big guy says in a deep, clear voice. "My name is Phelan Lone Star. What's your connection with the white buffalo?"

"We stopped by to pay our respects, like anybody else, get hired to drive it cross country."

"That's good," says Phelan Lone Star.

"How come you were trying to kidnap the buffalo?"

"We don't consider it kidnapping. Let me ask you this, are you guys Christian?"

"No!" we say emphatically.

"Well, you know lots of Christians, I bet. Suppose Christ came back like they been claiming he's going to for two thousand years? Suppose he was sold to one of the TV networks and made an appearance each week on Geraldo, or America's Funniest People? Do you think Christians would call it kidnapping if a few of them rescued Him and spirited him off to some holy, contemplative place where only true believers could visit him?"

"And you guys?"

"We feel the same about the white buffalo as Christians would about Christ," says Phelan Lone Star. "I'm a holy man among my own people."

"But you make lousy buffalo-nappers, right," says Frank, draw a smile from two out of three of them. Frank go on to explain who we are, and how they been trailing the wrong buffalo, and how we was fooled too, and bleached the wrong buffalo at our own expense . . .

"Where are you from?" Frank ask Phelan Lone Star and his friends.

He start to name a state, then he catch himself, stop and simply say, "The Southwest."

"What do you figure to do with the buffalo when you get him?" we ask.

"Keep him in a sacred place where only those who respect what he stands for will be able to visit him. See, what's happened is the buffalo been passed around a few times, the price going up and up, as the white men realize they got a gold mine on their hands. Near as we can tell he's owned by a corporation that also owns a TV network, whole thing might be owned by the Japanese. That corporation planning to tour him all over the world, charge whatever the traffic will bear.

"Well," says Frank, "as I say twenty time every broadcast of Brother Frank's Gospel Hour, 'What would it take to make you happy?' Let me know and Brother Frank will see what he can do."

"We want the buffalo, but that big corporation has pretty tight security. They already deked us out by having us follow you guys instead of the real white buffalo. We were so sure. We even had a spy on the inside."

"No one was more fooled than us. We believed everything they told us. We were scared that the real white buffalo was on its way to the packing plant. We believed it so much we spent half a day bleaching the other buffalo."

The light come shining on for all of us about the same time.

"Whitey is to arrive here at noon tomorrow. There's only one main highway. We just have to drive a couple of hundred miles down the road, spot them as they go by, follow them, and when they stop . . . "

Frank is jumping up and down he is so excited. Phelan Lone Star look serious while he contemplate the situation. His two friends, one is actually called Squat, and the other Billy, seem to look at us for the first time.

Frank's friendship with locks help us let ourselves into the barn where Chief Tom is resting. Frank start up the truck we drove before and we hook the trailer on it. I blindfold Chief Tom with a feed sack and he walk on board the trailer like a friendly dog.

We high tail it along the Interstate for a few hours, then turn around so we heading toward Fargo, stop at a truck stop where we can scan the Interstate. We plan to take turns sleeping, one person always keeping watch, but all of us are too excited to sleep.

It is while four of us are eating a very early breakfast that Squat come hot footing it into the restaurant.

"They just went by," he yells. We leave in a flurry of half-eaten food, and dollar bills scattered across the table for checks and tips.

"They'll have to stop for either gas or food before they reach Fargo," says Phelan Lone Star.

"We hope."

We try to stay at least a half mile behind, and we sure are happy when they turn off at the very next exit and in to a truck stop. We park right beside them. The trucks and trailers are identical.

"You guys get lost for a few minutes," Frank say to Phelan and company. "Me and Silas, we'll take care of everything."

"What are you gonna do?" Phelan ask suspiciously.

"Trust me," says Frank. "I know what I'm doing."

The last time Frank said that, Etta had to get Robert Coyote to drive her two hundred miles to put up our bail.

Me and Frank walk into the restaurant, moving right down the rows of booths until we spot the guys traveling with the truck.

"Boy, are we glad we caught up with you," says Frank, heave a big sigh. "Word has it that there a rest stop about ten miles up the road where these here renegade Indians plan to force you off the road, steal the white buffalo."

These guys know we were driving the decoy trailer, have no reason to doubt us.

"What Beau and James Earl told us to do is switch trailers with you. You guys just drive along leisurely, let yourselves be pulled over. Don't put up any fight. Let these renegade Indians take the truck and trailer. What they'll get is the brown buffalo. We'll come along a half hour behind you."

We even buy their breakfast, help them switch the trailers, wave them goodbye.

"I don't know how you did that without a fight," says Phelan Lone Star, "but I'll be grateful forever."

"My work here is done," says Frank, imitating the Lone Ranger. "Me and my faithful companion, Only His Nose Showing Above Water, are off to aid other worthy citizens in distress."

"If you ever want to visit the buffalo," says Phelan Lone Star, "I'll always know where it is, though it will be deep in the Indian Nation in the Southwest. Outsiders could never find it."

"You can always reach me," he go on. "Ironically, I have to earn a living. There's not much money in being a shaman these days. I wear a suit five days a week and operate Lone Star Furniture and Appliances in Flagstaff, Arizona. Send me a FAX sometime. Oh, and if you ever want a deal on a sofa or a microwave . . . "

"You think we been had?" Frank say to me after Phelan and company drop us off at the airport. "You figure the buffalo will be on display at Lone Star Furniture for five dollars a peek?"

"Only time will tell," I say.

The Auction

Because the Outcalt's farm backs up on the reserve the shortest way for them to get to Wetaskiwin is to cross Indian land. Nobody minds, and the Outcalt family, at one time there was eight kids, are pretty well known on the reserve. They shop sometimes at Ben Stonebreaker's General Store, buy gas at Fred Crier's Texaco garage, and over the years several of the kids hang around the Hobbema Pool Hall shooting snooker and drinking Coke. Stan, the oldest boy, who must be over thirty now, married one of the Crying-for-a-vision girls, Felicia, I think. They live in Wetaskiwin and both work for the Bank of Montreal.

The Outcalts are good people, work hard, none of them ever been in serious trouble. That's why it struck me as odd when Dwayne and Murray Outcalt have a drag-em-out fist fight in front of Ben Stonebreaker's Store in the middle of a Tuesday afternoon. No alcohol involved. Dwayne who is about my age, and the last boy still living on the farm, come out of the store breaking the cellophane off a pack of smokes, when Murray, who is a year or so older, pull up in his all-terrain vehicle got about an inch of mud on it. They say a couple of words to each other, that I can't hear, then Murray slam Dwayne in the belly with a hard right and the

30

battle is on. They roll down the steps of the store, through the mud and gravel of what pass for a street, cursing and pounding on each other.

Me, Frank Fencepost and Bedelia Coyote are sitting at the far end of the long low-slung steps to the store, Frank and Bedelia are eating Popsicles. The fight ain't none of our business so we just let them go on until they get tired. A few younger kids gather round, cheer one or the other, leap out of the way as the fight move first one direction them another. They finally stop, panting and cursing, covered in dirt and grass stains, blood running down Dwayne's face and out his nose.

Dwayne walk toward his pickup, toss a fistful of gravel at the all-terrain, make some chips in the windshield.

It is Bedelia who knows what the fight was all about. Bedelia seem to know everything, we call her our combination newspaper, radio and TV. Mrs. Outcalt died about three months ago, from cancer, Bedelia say. Mrs. Outcalt was a thin, quiet lady, who was nice to everybody. When I was in grade school she used to drive a purple Buick, and each time she'd shop at Ben Stonebreaker's she'd buy a handful of penny candies and hand them out to us kids who were hanging around on the steps of the store. These days, I sometimes do that. It is a pleasure to make kids happy. I remember that Ma and Mad Etta, our medicine lady, had Frank drive them to her funeral at a Baptist church in Wetaskiwin. There are only two of the Outcalt kids at home, Dwayne and a teenage girl, Vivian, who catch the school bus to Wetaskiwin at a too early hour in the mornings, even though she own a little red car that must cost twenty-five thousand, her dad won't let her drive it to high school. The family was close, all the other kids live nearby, Wetaskiwin,

Ponoka, Edmonton, and the older boys still work the farm with their dad.

The fight between Dwayne and Murray was over some of their mother's possessions. There are eight kids and not enough stuff to go around, or at least not enough to be divided so everybody get what they want, which Bedelia point out is a big difference.

"They all, or at least six or seven of them want the same things," says Bedelia. "I talked to Vivian at the bus stop one morning. It's just the usual stuff, a dresser set, a couple of rings, a favorite book, some fancy dishes. A couple of needlepoint pictures she made, photo albums, an ornament or two, some of her clothes. Her Bible," and Bedelia roll her eyes, and so do me and Frank.

"One of the sisters who live in Edmonton, says her mother promised her all the stuff and she walked it all out of the house right after the funeral. The other kids were so pissed off they went to her place when she was out and carried the stuff back home. The two oldest girls got in a hair-pulling match, and old man Outcalt was so furious he confiscated all the stuff and locked it up in his safety deposit box in Wetaskiwin. But their family is like rival groups of terrorists. The old man don't know who to believe or what to do about dividing up his wife's stuff."

"Pretty crazy," says Frank. "I'll suggest he donate the whole mess to Brother Frank's Gospel Hour. We'll make good use of it. I'll mention that on the air tonight. They should call on Brother Frank to solve their problems. In my capacity as mediator . . ."

"For goodness sakes," says Bedelia, really annoyed. Her tolerance for Frank has never been high, and it bothers Bedelia that Frank has almost accidentally become successful. Now, Bedelia, who always consider herself twice as smart as Frank and all his friends put together, works for him; he pays her well and she can afford to give money to all her Save The Whatever causes, still . . .

I was at Mad Etta's, whose real name is Margueretta Black Horses, the night Bruno Outcalt come to see her. We hardly ever call Etta, Mad Etta to her face, and those who forget themselves got the scars to remember their mistake. I once seen Frank Fencepost go head first through her screen door, do himself a certain amount of damage as he bounced down the rocky path from Etta's cabin.

Bruno Outcalt is a man in his late fifties, round of build, with a red face and blue eyes, under a John Deere cap with lots of oil on the bill and crown. He wear bib-overalls over a black knitted sweater. He been driving a cultivator in the Alberta spring wind for most of the day, and though he's washed up there are still smears of black loam around his eyes, and I bet if you was to slap him on the back he'd emit a great cloud of black dust. He smell of machinery, cigarettes and whiskey.

They greet each other like old friends. I never guessed they knew each other. Bruno pull a half-finished mickey of rye whiskey from his overalls, and Etta serve up cups of coffee from the blue enamel coffee pot that live like a pet on the back of her cookstove. The coffee is thick and bitter so a dollop of whiskey can't help but improve its flavor.

Bruno look me up and down for quite a while, until Etta give what could be a small smile, or a gas pain, say it is okay for him to talk in front of me because I'm her apprentice medicine man. It is nice to hear this, just to confirm what Etta has told me more than once over the years. I may be her apprentice but Etta ain't passed on all that many secrets of being a medicine man. I guess Etta got what would be called a universal affliction. She don't believe she's ever gonna die.

"I don't know what to do about them damn kids," Bruno says.

"Hmmph," says Etta which is her standard reply. She believe in just listening to what people got to say before she offer up any opinion.

"Stan's wife is the only one who has a lump of common sense in her, and I got to think maybe that's because she's Indian. I don't want to sound out of line here, but I heard stories about how in the old days when one of your people died the family not only gave away the dead person's possessions, but they gave away all of their own possessions and started life fresh. My kids have chosen up sides, they're greedy and spoiled. Instead of grieving together, they're fighting like mink. Felicia, Stan's wife, says we should remember Magdelaine in our hearts, that possessions aren't things to be argued over."

"Felicia Crying-for-a-vision always been a smart girl," says Etta from the shadows, where she sit up high in her treetrunk chair.

"What do I do? I'm pissed with these kids. I lost my wife of forty years, I could use a little support, instead of them quarreling like magpies over a carcass."

"Anything they fighting over very expensive?" ask Etta.

"Naw. Her birthstone ring is worth maybe two hundred dollars. If I hear the words *sentimental value* one more time I'm gonna trash the whole lot, run them kids off the farm, tell them they ain't welcome back until they smarten up."

"They each want to believe your wife loved them most," say Etta.

"Well, she didn't. She loved 'em all the same."

"Hmmph," said Etta again, with more emphasis. She eyed the whiskey bottle on the table. Bruno stood up walked the few feet to her chair and poured the last couple of ounces into her cup.

I realize that Bruno Outcalt is older than I thought, probably closer to seventy. He has an old man's gait. When he take off his cap, his snow-white forehead run clear to the back of his head. He might be close to Etta's age. Though how old Etta is, is anybody's guess. Ma, who's over fifty, says Etta was old when she was a girl. Another time I heard Etta was only sixty-five. Somebody else said she was a hundred.

"Let me think on it for a couple of days," says Etta. Then she sympathize some with Bruno Outcalt, for the loss of his wife and for having ungrateful children. That seem to make him feel a bit better. Something Etta has taught me is that people feel better if you agree with them, even when you don't exactly mean it.

"What would you do?" Etta ask me soon as the door to her cabin close. I hate it when she asks me questions like this. It is worse than taking an exam at school. It must be what an intern feels like while on rounds with a doctor, an intern who was out with his girlfriend the night before and not studying his *Gray's Anatomy.*

I stall as long as I can. "I think I'd take them down to Hammersmith's Gym in Wetaskiwin, tell the guys to put on the gloves and go for it; I'd have the girls wrestle."

Etta look at me like I'm something she just wiped off her boot.

"What if one of the girls was arguing with one of the boys?"

"Okay, so my idea isn't very good. And there are eight of them. It might not be fair for the strongest one to win."

"Hmmph," says Etta.

"Mr. Outcalt could number all the stuff, and the kids draw for it."

"Soon as that was done they'd start trading back and forth and soon they'd be fighting again."

I try a couple more ideas, including one that Mr. Outcalt should collect everything that been argued over and cut each item into eight parts.

"You're getting closer," says Etta. "That would end the conflict alright. Keep thinking on it, Silas, and come back two nights from now when Bruno Outcalt pays his next visit."

I did. I think Etta was disappointed Bruno didn't have a mickey stashed in his overalls the second time.

"They're getting worse," he said. "Vivian and Dwayne got to cursing each other out this morning at breakfast. I didn't know my little girl knew such language. Emma, the one who lives in Ponoka, says she's going to hire a lawyer to see she gets what's coming to her."

"She ain't talking about money, is she?" says Etta.

"No, she ain't."

"You figure yourself for a rich man?" Etta ask.

Bruno Outcalt take a while to answer. "There's different kinds of rich. I'm like most farmers, land and machinery poor . . ."

"But I hear you buy cars for your kids, the stationwagon for Stan and his family, the fancy off-road for Dwayne, that cute little red car for Vivian."

"Yeah, I done that."

"I'm just trying to figure how rich you are, without asking to look at your pass book from the Bank of Montreal. If I said it would cost exactly sixteen thousand dollars to solve your problem, what would you say?"

"I'd say cheap at twice the price," said Bruno Outcalt.

"Good," says Etta. "Here's what you do."

On the night of the auction me and Frank drive Etta up to Wetaskiwin in Louis Coyote's pickup truck. Me and Bedelia each have leased a really nice car with the salary we make from Brother Frank's Gospel Hour, and Frank have a Lincoln that is big as both of ours put together. But the place Etta fit best is in her tree-trunk chair in the back of Louis' old truck that, if it has any original parts left, probably first hit the road about 1947. Frank offered to replace Louis' truck, but Louis, who been blind for about fifty years, says he can't see no reason to do that. "As long as the wheels turn, don't matter to me what it looks like," says Louis Coyote with a sly smile.

We take off the buffalo robe that cover Etta, help her down off the truck, then carry her chair into the auction house, guide Etta in after it. There is a platform at the front and about fifty yellow wood folding chairs in maybe seven rows. The platform and all along the sides and back of the room are stacked with furniture and used household stuff. Mr. O'Hara will work himself from the platform all around the room, selling as he goes.

What Etta told Bruno Outcalt to do was gather up all the stuff that been fought over, call each of the kids and ask if there was anything they wanted added to what's in the safety deposit box. He tell them everything in it going to be auctioned off at O'Hara's Auction House in Wetaskiwin, two weeks from Wednesday.

"After that you write each child a check for two thousand dollars. They'll each have that and only that to bid with, the one who manages their money most carefully will be most likely to get what they want."

"Boy, I bet there gonna be some wild bidding," I say to Etta after Bruno Outcalt gone on his way.

"Hmmph," say Etta again, could have any of a half dozen meanings.

The auction only been going on for fifteen minutes when the Outcalt stuff come up. Mr. O'Hara start off with a tea pot, a fancy green and white one of thin china that I known to be real expensive. I even handled one once at Reed's China and Gift Shop in Edmonton. The tea pot is made of Beleek or by Beleek, I not sure. After a few bids he get the price up to twenty dollars, only a couple of antique dealers stay in the running. The tea pot go to one of them for a hundred and fifty dollars, which is about half what it's worth in a store. I look over at Bruno Outcalt, where he's leaning on an old piano, his black reflection staring back at him; he has his John Deere cap off and is scratching his fringe of white hair.

After the second item also go to an antique dealer, I start to seriously stare around the auction house. I bet there are two hundred people jammed into the chairs and standing all along the rows of furniture and appliances. The place is smoky as a bingo hall. The birthstone ring ain't drawing much in the way of bidding. I keep staring around. I am real surprised for try as I might, I can't spot any of the Outcalt kids. I look at the back of the room, where Etta, in the shadows, is sitting way up on her tree-trunk chair. Etta is smiling.

The Lightning Birds

That summer it was impossible to get a job. Things was so bad I end up working on a farm for a guy named Wilf Blindman. He got a big farm down to the south end of the reserve and I bet he is the richest Indian in the area, in money anyway.

I don't like to work on a farm. I been taking courses at the Tech School in Wetaskiwin on how to fix tractors, but I never even sniffed a job doing what I been trained for. Working for Wilf Blindman I get to cut clover with a team of horses and a mower, and after its cut I get to make coils of hay in the field with a shiny-tonged pitch fork.

It is pretty lonely work. Wilf is the kind of guy who says "Yep", or "Nope", after you ask him a question. And if he strains himself and says, "Looks like rain," that amount of conversation likely to last him for two or three days. I miss my girlfriend, Sadie One-Wound, and my friends, Frank Fencepost and Rufus Firstrider. Wilf's farm is too far off the beaten track to walk anywhere of an evening, and usually I'm too tired anyway. Wilf only let me off on Sundays, and then on the condition, "You don't have none of your useless friends hang around steal everything that ain't nailed down."

Wilf may be an Indian, but he think like a white man. I guess you have to do that to be successful. Wilf left his bank book sitting out on the table one evening and I seen he got enough money in the Bank of Montreal in Wetaskiwin to last somebody like me a couple of lifetimes. He could afford farm equipment if he wanted. But then horses work for food and I practically do too. Coal oil lamps and a wood stove is cheaper than electricity. Maybe Wilf ain't got the wrong approach after all.

About two weeks after I got there, while I'm eating supper with Wilf, canned Campbell's Soup, with bread and margarine — Wilf sure don't waste any money on food, for either him or me — Wilf say to me, "Kid's comin' to visit."

"What kid?"

"Brother's kid. Girl. His wife's dead." That about broke Wilf's record for speaking words in a row.

Next morning Wilf open up the door to a small bedroom off the kitchen.

"Clean it up," he says.

Take me most of the day. There is a single bed, an old dresser with a mirror so yellow and spotted it like staring into rippling water. The room is filled with junk. Boxes might have come from an auction, some full of old magazines, other got dead flashlights, parts from vacuum cleaners, cracked dishes. There is harness strewn around, some coyote hides in the corner. Whole place ain't been dusted in my lifetime.

Wilf is a tall, ungainly man with a slight stoop. He have bushy eyebrows, and a square, clean-shaven face, look like polished oak. He shave every morning with a shaving mug and a straight razor, after he pump a washbasin full of cold water from the cistern under his house.

His house is tall and unpainted, gaunt windows stare across the prairie. Coming down the road toward Wilf Blindman's place, if I didn't know someone lived there I'd think the house been vacant for years.

The child that arriving must have something to do with a letter Wilf got the second day I was working for him. The mailman, one of the Dodginghorse boys, is probably a cousin of Wilf's if you was to check back far enough. Instead of leaving the mail in the mailbox at the end of what must be a quarter mile driveway, he drive his Canada Post car right to Wilf's door, give letters to him in person if he's there, otherwise put them under a rock that sit on the front porch.

Wilf sat at the kitchen table what covered in a gray oil-cloth, got black squiggles all over it, fit right in with the darkness of the whole place, and read the letter by the wavery light of a gas lamp, again and again. Wilf could afford light, but I think he enjoys living a dark life like a mole.

There was a good old Alberta thunder and lightning storm raging outside, lightning zippering across the sky, now and then frying a tree somewhere not far away, thunder rattling the window panes. Didn't look like Wilf was one to make quick decisions. Look to me like he is as stolid and silent as the land he farms.

"What do you know about Wilf Blindman?" I ask Etta our medicine lady the next Sunday when I'm back at Hobbema.

Etta don't waste any words either.

"Got his heart broke twenty years ago. Lives like a hermit. Don't want anyone to forget he got his heart broke. Better at feeling sorry for himself than anybody I know. Probably gone bushed from living out there alone for so long."

"How'd he get his heart broke?"

"Same as anybody else. He loved a girl; she married some-body else. Only difference everybody else sulk around for a week or two, or a month or two then get on with their lives. Wilf still sulking."

"Must have loved her a lot?"

"Hmmmph!" says Etta. "He enjoy being a victim. Made a career out of it. Listen, unless you being held hostage, or got a terminal illness, what you got in life is pretty much what you want."

I'm gonna try to remember that.

"Yeah," I say. "Kitchen floor at Wilf's is so dirty people wipe their feet when they get outside."

But I changed all that. I sluiced out the kitchen, washed down the walls. I took the bedding off the bed and the curtains off the windows in what I think of as the guest room. There is no kind of washing machine on the place so I get permission to drive Wilf's truck to the laundromat in Wetaskiwin, and reluc-tantly, a ten dollar bill to change into quarters.

The blankets and sheets wash up okay, but the curtains which was made from what look like yellow lace, break up in a thousand pieces in the wash, look like I been laundering Kleenex.

I price some curtains at Field's Department Store.

Back at the farm, Wilf stare at me like I'm trying to rob him. But I remembered to toss a double-handful of what was left of the curtains into the truck box.

"Look like mush I could feed the chickens," Wilf says and almost smile. He pull out a sweaty-looking roll of twenties and peel off money for curtains.

I would have liked to suggest a toy or a doll or something bright for a little girl. Everything around Wilf's farm is in black and white. But, I figured I inconvenienced Wilf enough already. I get bright blue curtains, with pink kittens running all across them. Bet the bedroom is in shock to have so much color in it at one time.

"Hello, I'm Jennifer Chickadee," the little girl says, soon as she step down out of the mouth of the north-going bus.

She is thin with gangly arms and legs, at the age where she's growing new front teeth; she is about as ugly as she's ever gonna be, and that's still pretty. Her hair is in a long braid, tied with a blue ribbon; her skin is the soft, light color of buckskin. Her nose is straight, her eyes hazel, and in spite of her missing teeth she have a very beautiful mouth. In five years she's gonna drive a lot of boys crazy.

"Hi, I'm Silas," I say.

If I hadn't been there I don't know what Wilf would have done. He stand back about twenty feet from the front of the bus, look like he got the worries of the world on his shoulders.

The bus driver hand me Jennifer's suitcase from underneath the bus. We walk back toward Wilf.

"Hello, I'm Jennifer Chickadee," she say to him.

"Hyuh," says Wilf, don't make to hug her or even shake her hand.

"You look just like my father," the little girl says.

Wilf grunt again and turn to walk toward the truck and parking lot, leaving me with Jennifer.

I ain't gettin' paid enough for this, I think.

I do have a young sister, Delores.

"You like Barbie dolls?" I ask after she climb up on the seat between me and Wilf.

That get her started. She tell me all about her dolls, and if her suitcase wasn't in the truck box she would have showed me the one she brought with her.

What I'm wondering is if she's Wilf's brother's child, how come she's named Chickadee and not Blindman?

Wilf sit behind the wheel like he's frozen, concentrate on shifting the gears, glance quick at Jennifer a few times, but never say even one word.

"Brother changed his name," Etta say to me. "Decided he didn't want to be Indian no more. Al Lindman used to be Alphonse Blindman. Hear he's a big car dealer in Calgary."

"How come her name's Chickadee?"

"Why don't you ask her? In case you ain't figured it out, was her mother broke Wilf Blindman's heart. Her mother was Sylvia Born With Long Hair. She was Wilf's girlfriend. Wilf's old man, Seymour Blindman, when he knew he was going to die, called both boys together, said there wasn't enough farm for both of them. Wilf wanted to stay on the farm, so he did. Alphonse took the money from a little life insurance policy, worth way less than the farm, and head off to Calgary.

"He buy himself a couple of old cars, fix them up, paint them, and sell them. Pretty soon he rent a lot on a main street, have Al's Premium Used Cars. It was about that time he cut off his braids, dress like a white man, change his name to Al Lindman.

"Al come back to the reserve one Christmas, take off back to Calgary after a week or so with Sylvia.

"Like I said, Wilf been sulking ever since. Al just keep getting more and more successful. He supposed to have his fingers in a dozen or so pies, besides his Chrysler/Plymouth dealership, like insurance companies, and I hear one of his companies build highrise apartment blocks.

"About three years ago Sylvia up and died. That's when Wilf go from just being an old bachelor to being a hermit and a strange one at that.

"I went out to the farm once, you know. I get Rider Stonechild to drive me there. I try to tell Wilf that feeling sorry for yourself is a pretty poor way to spend your life. But he blames Al for Sylvia dying. He thinks he didn't treat her right. Says he's gonna get even, whatever that might mean. The Blindman brothers was never close, but I don't think they spoke a word in the fifteen years since Al stole Wilf's girl.

"Wilf ain't near as old as he looks. You should see Al, looks like he could be Wilf's son. Al ain't a bad guy. Word around is he offered Wilf a good job, but Wilf turned him down. Then he offered Wilf an interest free loan to develop the farm. All Wilf said was, 'Got my own way of doin' things.' What I can't figure out is why a rich man like Al Lindman send that poor little girl for Wilf to look after. You got to stick around there, Silas, make sure that she's okay."

I been complaining all evening I wish I could find any kind of a job so I could get away from Wilf and his farm.

If I ever seen a little girl dying for somebody to like her, it is Jennifer Chickadee. But Wilf is perfect at ignoring her. It is like she hasn't arrived yet.

One lunch time when me and Wilf comes in from the hay field, Jennifer has added wood to the fire box, heated up Campbell's Chicken Noodle soup, and made us each a bologna sandwich. She even set the kettle to boiling tea water.

Because Wilf don't say nothing, I go overboard praising her cooking. I stare at Wilf, my look telling him to say something nice. All he do is wipe the sweat off his forehead with his hand, dry his hand on his overalls, give Jennifer a longer than usual glance, as if he trying to decide exactly what it is of his she's stolen.

I read where someone said that dealing with Indians is like trying to play catch with someone who won't throw the ball back. Wilf won't even catch the ball let alone throw it back.

Another few days and I get around to talking to Jennifer. "Is Chickadee your real name?"

"I figured if I was coming to live with a real Indian, I should have an Indian name," is what Jennifer says. "I thought about being Blindman like Uncle Wilf, but Chickadee is prettier. My Daddy used to say I was like one of those bouncy little black and white birds. I wish I could remember more about my mother. I was five when she died, and she is kind of like a character in a TV show I watched a long time ago. I have a picture of her, but I can't remember her actually touching me.

"Daddy's told me a hundred times at least never to mention I'm Indian. He says we're Irish, Black Irish. And I heard him tell one of his friends that Mama was from Quata-malla. I don't understand what's wrong with being Indian. Daddy says people won't like us if they know we're Indian.

"Do people not like you, Silas? I guess people don't like Uncle Wilf. He sure doesn't seem to have any friends."

This summer there are a record number of thunder and lightning storms. Almost every night the huge black cloud billow up out of the west like black ships and the lightning crisscrosses the sky like gold chains. The wind swirls, the trees bend and the rain begins with a few plopping drops that make quarter-sized impressions in the yard dust, then the rain turns to a torrent, slams against the windows and beats the dandelions flat to the ground. Thunder shakes the whole house, and we can hear the whine of lightning and the crash and screech as it strikes. Once it hit a lone aspen out by the county road, split it almost in two. Sometimes we can't do much work the next day because everything is so wet. There are storms in the afternoons too. Me and Wilf have to come in from the fields and we sit and watch the windows steam up. We play three-handed Snap, and Books, and Hearts. Wilf don't act like he enjoying himself. Soon as the rain stop he pulls on his rubber boots and slogs off toward the barn.

Another week passes. There is something weird going on here. I wish I knew what it was, and if I should be worried enough about it to tell Etta or somebody else. I sure would hate for something to happen to that little girl.

Frank Fencepost come by to visit one evening. He take a shine to Jennifer right away.

"Guess who gives the orders in a cornfield?" says Frank. "The Kernel," he answer before Jennifer had a chance to think about the question. She smile showing the big gaps between her teeth.

"I have a photogenic memory," Frank says, showing Jennifer how he can read something once, even upside down and then repeat it all back. The joke goes over her head, but I laugh and explain it to her.

"The bank's looking for teller," Frank says.

"I thought they just hired one last month," I say, playing along.

"That's the one," says Frank, slap his thigh. Jennifer giggle and bounce around the kitchen like she was on a pogo stick. Wilf sit at the kitchen table, glare into a three month old copy of the *Western Producer*.

Jennifer is a city girl all the way. She at first can't believe we don't have indoor plumbing. She never even guessed there were outhouses. Or wood stoves. Or houses without electric light. I'm guessing she don't even know her mother was Indian, or that she have maybe a dozen relatives with the same name as her mother, Born With Long Hair, on the reserve, and I bet hundreds of cousins in Southern Alberta on the Blood Reserve, where her mother's family come from originally. Etta says Sylvia Born With Long Hair was light skinned and had gray eyes. I'm afraid if I tell Jennifer she has relatives on the reserve Wilf will fire me and I won't be able to keep an eye on Jennifer.

A few days ago Wilf started talking. First he ask Jennifer if she'd like to ride on the cultivator with him, and she act like he's taking her to Disneyland. She spend all day with Wilf, while I'm mending fences. She come in sunburned and covered in black dust. She lines up behind Wilf to wash her hands in the white enamel washbasin sit on a upturned apple box over by the cream separator.

"Uncle Wilf told me stories all day," she says later on while we're sitting on the front steps. "But he says they're secret stories, and I can't even tell them to you, Silas."

I don't figure Wilf for the kind of guy to know any stories.

There is a weeping birch sit about a hundred yards south of the house, on a knoll in the pasture, alone like it been abandoned. One morning early I see Jennifer in front of the kitchen window, hands on hips, studying the tree, a scowl on her face.

"What?" I say.

"Uncle Wilf says that tree is where the lightning birds live. I've never seen any, have you?"

The tree is broken in several spots where it been struck by lightning before. If the tree were a man it would be walking on crutches.

I don't answer Jennifer's question. I've never heard of a lightning bird.

The next day Wilf and Jennifer go into town for a couple of hours. They come back with plain groceries—I'd been hoping for some gingersnaps, or Oreos, maybe a carton of ice cream we could sit right down and eat before it melted. What Wilf has sprung for is a yellow slicker and rainhat for Jennifer. She can't wait to try them on.

"Boy, I wish it would rain," she says, staring at the high, blue sky. She look like a giant cowslip running in circles around the weeping birch in the pasture. Wilf also bought her a child-sized broom which she wave like a weapon

"Soon as it rains I'm gonna put a scare into those lightning birds," Jennifer says.

I don't say anything.

"You ever heard of lightning birds?" I say to Etta soon as I get back to the reserve that Saturday evening.

"Uh-oh," says Etta. By her tone I know something is wrong. "That son of a bitch," says Etta. This from a big lady who hardly says anything stronger than oops!

"Tell me," I say. "Should I be worried? Jennifer's full of secrets these days," I say.

"Hard to know what he's up to. But I don't figure it for good. There's a legend, more a story. I don't know where it come from. Might even be a white man's story. There's these birds with silver and gold tails the color of lightning. When they set in a tree, or roost on the roof of a building the lightning finds them. I think the story is they got to be shooed away so the tree or house or building won't get struck."

"It's clouding up," Etta says to me, pointing out her window to where a thunderhead is peeking above the western horizon like a mountain.

"I seen something this morning," I say. "I can't believe I saw it, is why I wait so long to tell you. Just as the sun was coming up, I seen Wilf walk out to the weeping birch, stab a crowbar into the ground at the base of the tree. I can't believe Wilf would do something like that, send a little kid out in a lightning storm?"

"If he was mad enough at her father. If he didn't know what I know. I think you better run over to Louis Coyote's and see if you can borrow the truck."

"What is it you know?" I ask Etta, as we struggling to make a ramp with a couple of planks so Etta can make it up into the truck box.

The wind is picking up, the leaves are silverbacked, rustling dangerously. A dust demon whirls around my boots.

"I made a few inquiries," Etta say mysteriously. Etta makes these inquiries without ever leaving her cabin where she don't have a phone or a FAX or a computer. "Al Lindman's

51

dying. Maybe he knows, maybe he don't, but he senses it, that's why he's sent his girl to Wilf. The old saying's right, blood is thicker than anything else."

"I can't find the tarp," I say, as Etta and I try to wrestle her tree-trunk chair into the truck box. Etta is too big to fit in the cab.

"I been wet before," says Etta, ease herself down into the tree-trunk chair, both her and the truck sighing heavily.

"If Al Lindman senses trouble how come Wilf don't? Blood don't seem to mean much to Wilf."

Etta motion for me to drive.

The first big drops are plopping on the hood and I start the truck down the hill from Etta's cabin toward the highway. I drive like mad over the greasy country roads, the truck fishtailing in spite of Etta's weight in the back. It begins to storm in earnest, the wipers only partially clearing the windshield. The thunder is loud enough I can hear it over the roar of the truck, lightning zap across the sky in silver and yellow streaks.

The ditches are rivers. About a mile from Wilf's I have to slow down to pass the mail delivery truck which stopped on a piece of high ground, I guess waiting for the worst of the storm to subside. I catch a glance of Etta in the rearview mirror. She look like a muskrat just poke its head above water.

There is more trouble when I try to turn into Wilf Blindman's driveway. He have a sort of cattleguard made of poles, and the rushing water moved the poles apart enough for the front wheels to drop through. We come to a sudden stop. Etta's chair crash against the back window, teeter as it bounce back, look for minute like it might tip over.

The road for about half the distance of the driveway is under water. Up by the house on higher ground, I can see the old weeping birch, and through the wind and driving rain I can see Jennifer in her yellow slicker and hat, broom in hand, moving in among the tall grasses, standing guard against the lightning birds.

I open the door and step out into the deluge.

Etta is standing in the truck box.

"Run!" she hollers. "Get that little girl away from the tree."

I start out, take about ten strides when I hit a slippery spot, my feet shoot out from under me and I land right on my back in about a foot of running water. It take a few seconds for me to cough out the water, decide that nothing is broken, get to my feet and slither on. I slip to my knees one other time. I try hollering but sheets of rain and wind absorb the sound of my voice.

Jennifer is turned toward the tree so there's no chance of her seeing me.

I'm about half way there when Wilf Blindman burst from the door of the house come down the steps in one leap, a sheaf of papers flying from his hand and blowing away in the wind as he do. Wilf don't see me either. He scramble up the side of the ditch into the field, covering himself in mud in the process. He take a dozen long steps, sweep Jennifer up in his arms and turn away from the crippled tree. He cross to the ditch, Jennifer's little yellow hat falling and disappearing into the wind-blown grasses, and leap right into the flowing water making a big splash just as the lightning shrill across the sky again, kind of scream as it strike the base of the weeping birch, splitting it even worse than it was before.

The air is full of the stink of lightning. Thunder rattles the earth and the house seems to vibrate.

I get there in time to brace my feet extend a hand and help Will and his armful out of the ditch.

Jennifer is the only one of us laughing. She's got her arms locked around Wilf's neck. He is nuzzling her cheek, and both of them is so wet it hard to tell if the water on Wilf's cheek is rain or tears. He holds Jennifer tight and strokes her wet hair. He looks at her like he finally realizes what it is she's stolen from him. I'd guess it is something he can get along without.

Dangerous Consequences

There is somebody dead, somebody else in a lot of trouble, a lot of other people sad, angry, grieving. I have to take the blame for most of what happened, though I didn't have anything to do with the actual killing. Still, I'm responsible. I'm the reader among my group of friends, and if I hadn't been reading history, and if I hadn't shared what I read with my friends, nothing bad would have happened.

Something I should have learned by now is that weird customs can't be transplanted from one society to another. They can't even be transported from one generation to another, or one tribe to another. What may be acceptable behavior on one side of the street, may not be understood or tolerated on the other side.

What I read that caused such a furor was the history of a little town in Ontario. It wasn't very interesting until I came to an excerpt from the diary of a minister, written in 1812, describing a custom he called a "charivari", a custom that the minister said came to Ontario from Quebec. What excited me was that I guessed the custom had survived all these years, moved west, and had its name changed to shivaree.

Here in Alberta, a shivaree is something we Indians learn from the white man. It is an old custom where, after a wedding, friends and family follow the bride and groom home, stand around in their front yard, bang spoons on pots, pans and kettles, shout loud, sometimes sings songs like "Roll Me Over in the Clover".

Sometimes the newlyweds invite you in to continue the party, sometimes it is kind of an end to the evening where they serve coffee and cake while everybody calm down their excitement. Sometimes the married couple pay no attention and eventually the crowd break up and go home. What the shivaree does is show the people who get married that they have lots of friends. Everything always done completely in fun.

The "charivari" I read about was of a different kind, one for when a widow or widower got married. Guess those kinds were more common way back then when people didn't live so long.

In 1812 the people carry a coffin up to the door of the newlyweds, inside the coffin is someone from the community dressed up to represent the dead husband or wife. After the coffin set down on the door step the lid is opened and the "ghost" walked into the house and made demands on the newlyweds "for money or favors, which had to be dealt with," the minister wrote, "or mischief follows."

Unlike today, that crowd of friends and relatives wore fantastic costumes, dresses, masks, and sometimes they painted their faces. Wonder where they learned face-painting from?

The minister's story ended with a warning, one I read, understood, but didn't pass on to my friends when I told them about that custom. I should have paid a lot more attention to that warning: "Sometimes these rude intrusions are resisted and dangerous consequences follow."

Felice Jardin was one of those odd, quiet bachelors who keep to himself in his home on the reserve. He is probably a little over forty years old and lived all his life here at Hobbema. His father, like so many Indian men, disappear when he was a boy, and Felice grow up in a Department of Indian Affairs house at the end of Jump Off Joe Creek, with his mother, Fern, and goodness knows how many brothers and sisters, for they keep arriving at regular intervals even after the father left.

Felice was short and stocky with powerful legs and a barrel chest. He have a wide, round face with a lopsided potato nose, and large, dreamy eyes magnified by thick glasses. The Jardins were considered a pretty shiftless bunch, the boys were mean and wild, known to steal anything not nailed down, and were usually in jail by sixteen or seventeen, while the girls ran off with rodeo cowboys or oil workers soon as they looked old enough. I remember one of the younger girls was a Bernadette Jardin come to school for a few weeks while I was attending. She was a stump-like girl with long braids and a mean squint. I came up to her at recess, I had a green tennis ball I found and was going to ask if she wanted to play catch, but before I could say anything she threaten to beat the crap out of me, glare at me with nasty yellow eyes, so I turn my back and walk away. A few years later I read in the *Edmonton Sun* how a woman with that name been charged with murder for stabbing a man in a rooming house near the York Hotel, the big Indian bar in Edmonton. Not much doubt in my mind it is the same person.

Only Felice stayed behind. Fern Jardin drank a lot. She was a tall, bony woman, with high, sharp cheekbones, and a mean disposition. By the time the last kid moved on, and

Fern Jardin died of too much drink and not enough taking care of herself, only Felice was left.

What happen then was one of those little surprises in our life at Hobbema. Felice, who always been shy, only come out of the house to work in his garden, buy groceries at Ben Stonebreaker's Store, or attend a movie at Blue Quills Hall of a Saturday night, began to improve the place.

The house have masking tape holding the cracked window glass together, the warped siding show what left of some cherry-colored paint on it and the front steps pretty well rotted into the ground. The front yard is rutted dirt with a few dead appliances like leftover snow drifts, and what's left of a yellow, 1969 Dodge sunk to its axles in the soft earth.

With Felice there alone, things begin to change. One spring a hanging flower basket appear beside the front door and by July it expand and bloom with orange, red, and yellow nasturtiums, and purple petunias. The broken glass get replaced. Felice rebuild the front steps and replace the warped siding, then he paint, not in the bright colors Indian Affairs painted the other houses, but with heavy gray paint what was probably meant for boats or concrete floors.

After noticing the improvements, some of us remember that Felice always had a private vegetable garden where there was rows and rows of soccer-ball-sized cabbages and white splotches of cauliflowers, rows of peas and yellow beans staked out, a plot of cucumbers curled on the loamy earth, even a pumpkin or two.

Felice fence himself a front yard made of pickets about five feet tall, which he paint the same concrete-gray of the house. Flowers begin to appear all over the property. There are circular flower beds and triangular beds, and a gravel path to the front door, all banked with whitewashed stones.

There are hanging baskets full of colorful flowers flowing almost to the ground. There are white-painted barrels with bright red hoops, petunias spilling over the edges like purple and red chipmunks. He done the same in the backyard. There are lilacs that lean over the fence, their fat purple coils pungent as frying sausage. In among the vegetables are marigolds the size of tea cups, and banks of what they call cosmos in bright colors like children pushing out a school door.

In spite of the color he create, Felice himself remain as colorless. He wear concrete-colored work pants, a street-colored shirt, and a plain cap with a brown bill and no advertising on the crown. He barely have a word to say to anybody. If someone was to comment on his pretty flowers he smile shy and nod, kind of duck his head into his neck like he's embarrassed.

Felice carry on his fascination with color all year round. There is a mountain ash tree in the front yard, and the bright orange berries illuminate the yard like Christmas lights. He also grow everlasting daisies, which he dry indoors, then he place little bouquets in the snow of his yard, so the kids who stand in their ragged parkas with their noses between the frosty pickets, staring at the daisies, think there are flowers growing up through the snow.

Felice never worked at a job that I know of. He take his government money, budget it real careful, never own a car, never waste a dollar on drink or drugs like so many people do. Felice probably would of lived like that forever if Florence Piche hadn't come home.

After about their third date, Florence Piche say of Felice, "You know what he told me? Said I can't smoke in his house, or even on his property. Bad for his plants. If I want a cigarette I got to go on the other side of the fence, outside the garden gate. If I figure to keep seeing him, guess I'm gonna have to quit."

And she did. Florence had a rough life of her own. She was raised here on the reserve, when she was a wild eighteen she married a rodeo cowboy name of Simon Piche and moved off with him to follow the rodeo circuit. Ten years, a divorce and a couple of kids later she come home. It ain't easy for her. She lived in the white world for so many years, now it's tough to be an Indian again.

Florence Piche always had a kind of spit in the face of the world attitude that I guess some would find attractive, and I'd also guess she had to develop that attitude to cope with all the grief she been through. Like most girls she was pretty as a teenager, though over the years she develop hard lines around her mouth, and a belligerent stare that lets everyone know she don't trust no one. I seen her one night in Wetaskiwin at the Canadian Legion, staggering drunk, and throwing punches at a big cowboy must have said something she didn't approve of. A bouncer got hold of each arm and carried her out to the parking lot.

It is about her second month back on the reserve that she turn up on Felice Jardin's doorstep carrying a box of asters she buy at the Safeway Garden Shop in Wetaskiwin, ask for advice on how to make them grow.

"Opportunist," is the word Etta, our four hundred pound medicine lady use to describe Florence.

"She'd never look twice at a man like Felice if she wasn't desperate. She's a lot younger than him, and she's been down the road and back a few times. Felice never been further from home than Wetaskiwin, and while he ain't stupid, he's simple as a ten year old. A girl like that, even if she means well, going to bring him nothing but grief."

I'm surprised to hear Etta say that. Usually she's happy to see two lonely people get together.

"Felice is an odd little man," she go on. "Far as anybody know he hardly even talked to a girl let alone have a romance of any kind. I'm not sure he needs a wife, or even knows what to do with one. And if he does need a wife, it should be somebody who loves him for himself. I hear tell that Simon Piche she was married to was Métis, don't have no status on a reserve, and that Chief Tom and Samantha investigating whether Florence should be allowed to move back here permanent. If Florence Piche can marry an Indian, and soon, she can stay on the reserve forever."

I guess Florence clued Felice in to quite a few things he wasn't so sure of. Florence's car, with the kicked in driver's door and missing back fender is parked overnight in front of Felice's place quite often. They turn up together at the Saturday night movie at Blue Quills Hall and sit, holding hands, Florence's head resting on Felice's broad shoulder. We even seen her giving Felice a driving lesson, though I don't think it took. But one day Florence, her kids and Felice drive off for the West Edmonton Mall, come back loaded with packages, and a trunk full of bedding plants. And, Florence wearing a thin gold engagement ring with a tiny diamond glinting in it.

Ken Many Beavers, a guy who don't often hang around with our gang, is the one who take most to heart the stories I tell everyone about the shivaree. Ken is a year or two older than most of us, and he drink more than we do, and is loud and obnoxious a lot of the time, even when he isn't drinking. Ken dated Julie Scar's sister, Bobby-Jean, for a couple of months was how he came to hang with us at all. After they break up he still invites himself along when we go to movies, hockey games, or just for a few beers at the Alice Hotel.

When Ken hear that Florence Piche and Felice Jardin going to get married at the end of the month he start gathering materials from his job site where he frame houses for Can-West Construction.

"Gonna build one hell of a coffin. I figure being divorced is about the same as being widowed. I even remember that Simon Piche she was married to. He had crow-colored, shoulder length hair and wore a yellow cowboy hat that must have cost two hundred dollars, all day every day."

Looking back, this is the point where I should have stepped in and said the whole coffin business wasn't such a good idea. I'm probably the only one besides Mad Etta who has had the experience of people not appreciating customs that ain't part of their culture.

But I don't step in and Ken Many Beavers build a coffin, which he store in the weeds behind Hobbema Pool Hall.

A wedding is always an occasion in a small community, so most all of us dress up and attend. Father Alphonse do the ceremony. Florence Piche wearing a bride's dress I seen in the window of the Second Time Round Shoppe in Wetaskiwin, and Felice Jardin, a couple of inches shorter than her wears a tuxedo he rented, make a small, stocky man like him look just like a penguin.

Florence have two sisters as bridesmaids, and one of their husbands is best man. Her little girl who is brown as fall grasses, is flower girl, and her son who has raven-black hair like his daddy, but close-together eyes like his mama, carry the ring. None of Felice's many brothers and sisters is there, which is just as well. After the ceremony there is a light supper at Blue Quills Hall, then everyone rest up for the dance that night.

Frank Sixkiller's band, Land Claims, play up a storm, and everybody seem to have a good time. There ain't that many presents on the table on the stage, for neither party have many friends, and a lot of people figure they got everything they need what with Felice having such a nice house and all. I admit I was one of the ones who didn't buy a present.

Etta sit in the shadows at the back of the hall on her tree-trunk chair, sip a rye and 7 that I fixed for her, look like one of those pictures you see in books of a storm cloud with a face.

As the dance winding down, and the best man about to drive the happy couple home, Ken Many Beavers and several of my friends including Frank Fencepost and Rufus Firstrider and Robert Coyote, go charging off toward the pool hall to retrieve the coffin. Ken is the only one really drunked up; his breath is strong enough to bend a wrench as he shouting out instructions and getting everybody together. They got a guy I hardly know, Mark Bend, to play the corpse. He wearing a black wig they borrowed from Connie Bigcharles, Frank's girlfriend, and Mark wear a yellow cowboy hat the way Florence's husband used to.

After giving the newlyweds time to get home a whole group of us start walking down the road toward Jump Off Joe Creek and Felice's house. Six guys carry the coffin on their shoulders and almost everyone is shouting and singing and generally having a silly time. At the foot of the hill below Felice's, Mark Bend get into the coffin, amid more joking and laughter. There are a couple of bottles being passed around.

"What's the matter with you?" my girlfriend Sadie One-Wound says to me, she bend her chin down toward her neck as she light a cigarette.

"I'm just not sure this is a good idea," I say.

"Geez, Silas, you're gettin to be a real spoil sport."

I don't figure there's much point in explaining my second thoughts.

Megan Coyote, the fiddler in Land Claims, strike up a jig tune and everybody move up toward Felice's house. There is a light on toward the back of the house.

When we get to the yard, we gather in front of the picket fence and everybody begin beating spoons or sticks on tin cans or pans or whatever been brought along. Most everyone has a flashlight or a lighter so the road look like it full of giant fireflies. Some of us point the flashlights at the sky and all those crisscrossing beams make things spookier than ever. I have a bad feeling about this whole situation. I'm hoping this will be one shivaree where the happy couple ignore their guests.

It is Ken Many Beavers who open the gate. Everyone pour into the yard, in the process some of the flower beds get tramped on, and I see a white stone rolling to the center of the grass from it been kicked from along the pathway.

Ken and his crew set the coffin down the doorstep. Ken pound with his fist on the aluminium storm door with the letter J set in a circle in the middle, that Felice bought at the M. D. Muttart Lumber Co. in Wetaskiwin.

Most of us is singing a rowdy song, and playing the flashlight beams across the front windows.

Eventually, the inside door open and Felice and Florence Jardin stand there. With the bluish light behind them they look pale as ghosts. Florence try to put on a smile, but she look nervous.

"We got somethin here for you," yell Ken Many Beavers. "Open up the door so's you can see."

Reluctantly, Felice unsnap the catch and push open the storm door. Soon as he do, Ken and his friends push the coffin right up to the entrance. Felice and Florence look scared and puzzled at the same time. I can feel my stomach dropping as I realize neither of them have a clue about the custom being enacted in front of them.

"See here, who's comin to visit you?" Ken Many Beavers says.

Somebody open the coffin, and just like from a vampire movie, Mark Bend sit up slowly. He wearing a cowboy's denim jacket, the yellow cowboy hat and the wig of long black hair. One of the girls has smeared lipstick on his face to look like blood.

Florence Piche take one look at him and faint dead away.

Felice get the most horrified look on his face, glance down at Florence, turn and run into the back of the house.

"I think we better get out of here," Ken says. But the people behind don't see what has happened. Megan Coyote is still fiddling away. People are yelling and singing, pounding on pots and pans.

What quiet everyone for a second or more is the blast from the shotgun.

Felice fire right through the glass part of the storm door. He don't aim at anybody. Just fire the gun. Mark Bend was just climbing out of the coffin and he take the full blast right in the rib cage. A few pellets hit Ken in the chest and side of the head, and about six other people pick up a pellet or two.

There is that second of dead silence as the echo of the blast fade away like thunder, then there is screaming and everyone is running out of the yard, people jam up at the gate and the pressure break away part of the fence.

When the RCMP get there, the flashers whirling blue and red, Constable Greer and Constable Bobowski find Felice sitting on the sofa in his living room, holding his bride. He hand Constable Greer the gun. Both of them was in shock, Constable Greer tell me the next day.

The ambulances take longer since they have to drive down from Wetaskiwin. Mark Bend is dead. Ken Many Beavers gonna look forever like he suffered the smallpox.

The investigation will go on for weeks, Constable Greer tell me, though the chances of any charges being filed against Felice Jardin are slim and none.

"I'm the one who caused it," I tell Constable Greer.

"It wasn't your fault, Silas. It was just a series of misunderstandings, and bad judgment."

"But if I hadn't read all that historical stuff . . . "

"You told a story based on fact. You're not responsible."

"But isn't it kind of like printing up directions for making a bomb and then being surprised when somebody actually makes a bomb?"

We talk this way for quite a while.

"It was just a combination of bad luck and bad judgment," says Constable Greer. Felice frightened easily, Florence was stressed out, had had a few drinks.

Though Mark Bend wasn't a friend of mine, he is still dead, and he wouldn't have been if I'd paid attention to that warning: dangerous consequences follow.

Hide and Seek

"The law is like rope," Etta our medicine lady says, "useful, necessary, strong, but it can be bent and twisted into all kinds of shapes depending on the occasion."

"What you're saying is there's two sides to every story?"

"Sometimes a dozen sides," says Etta. She is sitting on her tree-trunk chair at the back of her cabin, the place where she does her best thinking, and where she looks most intimidating.

We've been discussing a case that going to court tomorrow in Wetaskiwin, one where Etta been called to testify. Things look pretty bad for the guy who's been charged. His last name is the same as mine, Ermineskin. His first names are Delbert James, people who know him call him by both his first names at once. We don't consider ourselves related though I suspect generations ago we was cousins.

Delbert James is charged with kidnapping, forceable confinement, child endangerment, and if his little girl, Carmen, dies, which seem pretty likely, then he'll be charged with murder. There some other charges, too, pointing a rifle, stalking his ex-wife, and three or four more. Tomorrow deals only with kidnapping.

Reading that list of criminal charges make Delbert James look like a full time criminal, truth is he's a guy who's never been in trouble of any kind. He is one of those live-off-the-land Indians, took his family away from Hobbema and the reserve and civilization over ten years ago. His group live in the wilderness, hunt and trap, barter hides and home made goods for necessities, refuse to take any kind of help from the white man, or give anything back. While me and my friends ain't pioneers enough to join a group like that, we wish them well, respect what they want to accomplish, even though we often make jokes about them.

The trouble started way back when little Carmen Ermineskin, who was born out there in the wilderness, took sick. These back-to-the-land people don't believe in white man's medicine, so they treat her at home and when that don't work they have their own medicine man, Thomas Many Mountains, treat her with herbs and roots, medicinal teas, and a sweat-lodge visit. Finally, there is a dance ceremony where the whole community dance around this seven-year-old who has suddenly become pale and weak, can't walk by herself and get smaller every day.

"Old Many Mountains treat her with eleven herbs and spices just like Col. Sanders," says Frank Fencepost. "He also got a secret sauce he spread all over her make her extra-crispy.

"He's truly the fast food restaurant of medicine men," Frank go on. "Before he joined these back-to-the-land people he'd never doctored anything but other people's drinks." Thomas Many Mountains had been a part-time bartender at the Travelodge Motel lounge in Wetaskiwin.

Frank, as they say, shouldn't be calling the kettle black. He could be accused of being the fast food restaurant, *People*

Magazine, USA *Today*, of traveling radio and TV evangelists. And he has been.

"At least Many Mountains held a job. What did you ever do before you lucked into religion?"

"I contemplated," Frank says with a straight face. "Unless you're born a mystic, you got no idea how difficult contemplation is. No time for worldly jobs, I spend all my life contemplating on the mysteries of the universe."

"Like where was your next drink coming from."

Frank, he's combined Indian medicine, quick-fix psychology, and rant-and-rave Christianity to increase the standard of living for him and a few friends, including me, while, because Bedelia Coyote the resident social conscience in our group insists, we provide help to a lot of people that really need it. I even write up a column that get printed in quite a few newspapers where we give away Brother Frank's Gospel Hour money to people who write in their requests.

"This guy's watched too many Walt Disney movies," Frank says when he sees Delbert James Ermineskin in the prisoner's box, what made of polished oak and have a way of making even large men look small. What Frank means is that Delbert James dressed like a poor cousin to an actor in a Disney wilderness movie where the hero is always dressed in perfect furs and buckskins, his clothes clean and untorn even after a half-hour fight with a grizzly bear, not to mention that he's still got all his arms and legs and other important appendages.

Delbert James wear his long hair in two greasy braids tied with string. His clothes consist of heavy wool pants and a home-made buckskin jacket glazed with dirt and stained with everything imaginable. He look like he been sleeping in the forest for years, which he has been, and even though me and Frank seated several rows away, we get a strong whiff of Delbert James, leather, sour sweat, and pine sap.

Usually when an Indian go on trial in the white court system his lawyer manage to get him a haircut and scrounge up a suit so the Indian look a lot like the guys who are prosecuting him.

"What do you call an Indian in a three-piece suit? The defendant," Frank often joke, though like many jokes it contain more truth than anything else.

Delbert James' lawyer, appointed by the court, look about sixteen and have the squeaky voice to prove it. His name is Byron West and he admit this is his first criminal trial as a legal aid lawyer. He request a jury trial and when that group all assembled, they look to me like the choir in a Pentecostal church, old, white and mean looking. I bet as close to out-door living any of these people experienced is a ride through Banff National Park and the Columbia Ice Fields in their Buick pulling an $50,000 trailer with a TV and microwave.

The first witness is Edith Ermineskin the wife of Delbert James. There is some question about whether she is a wife or not, for they wasn't married by the government but by the old man named Two Elk who founded this back-to-the-land group. The prosecutor, the judge, and Byron West all wrangle about this for at least an hour. Eventually, they decide she is a wife. Then they have to explain to her that she don't have to testify against Delbert James unless she want.

"I want to," she says. "I really want to," and she stare at Delbert James without one shred of love left in her eyes. She begin her testimony by telling how, after the medicine man and the tribal dance couldn't help little Carmen, she want to take her to a white doctor or hospital, but Delbert James won't let her. Edith Ermineskin was named Edith Cardinal when she was young, and she was raised in civilization, in Wetaskiwin, in a house that have a basement and with a gas furnace.

There is something wrong with this whole proceeding, but it take me a few minutes to decide what it is. Edith Ermineskin been testifying in English, in fact all the business has been conducted in English, while all this time Etta, seated on two oak chairs, sit side-by-side to the prisoner's box translating every word into Cree for Delbert James. When did Delbert James forget English? When he was a young man, before he hook up with these back-to-the-land people, he went to high school for at least one year and he work in the O.K. Tire Store in Wetaskiwin on weekends, speak English as good as the next guy.

"Delbert James tell me he'd rather let our daughter die than have her touched by a white doctor. Me, I don't care, if my little girl's sick I'll do whatever it takes. And I did. In the middle of the night I sneaked Carmen out of camp, drag her on a travois over twenty miles through the woods to a highway, flag down a Department of Highways truck who drive her to a hospital."

It was while Carmen was in the hospital, after she'd been there for three weeks and wasn't getting any better, that Delbert James appear one night, point a rifle at the nurses, force Edith out of the room, wrap Carmen in a moosehide robe and carry her away on foot while sirens are blaring and RCMP cars are running both ways on the main street of that small town, red and blue light flip-flopping in all directions.

Delbert James' lawyer who look as if he been dressed by his mother to attend a birthday party, do all the awful things lawyers on TV do when he cross-examine Edith Ermineskin.

He suggest, and try to get Edith to admit to it being her idea to move Carmen back into the bush because the hospital and doctors weren't doing her as much good as the medicine man had.

"Isn't it true that Mr. Ermineskin had your permission to take your daughter away from the hospital?"

"No."

"Isn't it true that you were unhappy with the progress your daughter was making at the hospital?"

Edith Ermineskin take a long time to think that over before answering.

"Yes."

"And since you brought her to the hospital you thought you'd look like a bad mother if you took her out of the hospital while she was still sick?"

Edith take even longer to answer this time.

"I don't understand."

The judge tell the lawyer to rephrase the question.

The cross-examination go on for a couple of hours, but my guess is the jury still think Delbert James is one bad dude.

Constable B. B. Bobowski of the RCMP take the stand and tell how her and a constable from Rocky Mountain House drive into the mountains in a 4-wheel vehicle until the terrain get too rough for it, then they canoe down a river until a rapids force them back onto land. They then walk at least ten miles to a trapper's line cabin where some elk hunters had seen smoke coming from the stove pipe. That was where they found Delbert James and Carmen.

"We watched the cabin all night. About 4:00 AM we stormed into the cabin, guns drawn and arrested Delbert James Ermineskin. The little girl was too weak to be moved so we radioed for the RCMP helicopter which managed to land about a half mile away and flew her to a hospital in Calgary."

The odd thing that the defence lawyer bring out in cross-examination was that when she was admitted to that hospital, Carmen's leukemia had already gone into remission, and that remission held up these last six months while everybody preparing for the trial. Delbert James, not having any money, get to stay in jail the whole time.

The prosecution call a guy named Carl Pheasant to testify. He's not somebody I know, though he was supposed to have had a band that played at rodeos and country weddings ten years or more ago. He testify that his band was called the Red Pheasants and that fifteen years or more ago Delbert James was their vocalist.

"Was Mr. Ermineskin able to speak and understand English?"

"Definitely," says Carl Pheasant. "Delbert James was like a lot of us guys, he speak English except with his parents. He didn't speak very good Cree."

The prosecution get permission from the judge to play a tape of the Red Pheasants from thirteen years ago, and we listen to Delbert James sing "Lovesick Blues", and a Johnny Cash song, "Give my Love to Rose". He sing those songs in good clear English.

I get a laugh out of Etta, who is always one to speak slow and careful, trying to translate those song lyrics into Cree.

"Mr. Pheasant," the prosecutor say, "do you think you could forget how to speak English."

"No way."

"Do you think there is any reason for Mr. Ermineskin to require a translator?"

Before he can answer Delbert James' little lawyer make an objection, but the prosecutor got his point across, that Delbert James is faking. And the jury smart enough to guess that if he's faking his ability to speak English, then he's likely faking everything else.

The judge is a young man, as judges go, only about forty. He lives in Wetaskiwin and coaches and sponsors a Pee Wee hockey team from the County Orphanage. It said he buys all the equipment himself, which at the cost of hockey equipment you'd need a judge's salary to afford.

The jury take only half an hour to find Delbert James guilty.

"Do you have anything to say before I pass sentence?" the judge ask.

"You wouldn't understand," Delbert James say, admitting he can both speak and understand English.

"I have a little girl the same age as your daughter. I'd like to understand your thinking. Were you being selfish and using your daughter to advance your social and political agendas, or did you at least think you had her best interests at heart?"

"If you seen your little girl was dying would you do everything in the world to help her?"

"Of course."

"Well, I love my little girl as much as any father. When she hugs my neck and giggles in my ear my heart expands like blowing up a balloon. I should probably let my wife take her to the hospital after our Indian medicine failed. I was wrong, because there was always a chance they'd be able to help her. But, they didn't. Here's what I figured. I thought, I'll take her into the bush, and I'll hide her so good that even death can't find her."

"Do you think what you did was right?"

"I had no choice. I didn't care about myself. I only wanted to save my baby."

"And while she was with you her leukemia went into remission?"

"She started to get better because death could no longer find her."

"Do you think he'll find her again?"

"If he does I'll hide her again, unless you lock me up so I can't help her."

The judge talk legal talk for a while, whereas, heretofore, and all that, but what he is saying is that things don't always appear the way they seem, something I've known most of my life.

"I'm going to postpone sentencing for one year," the judge say. "This seems to be a case, Mr. Ermineskin, where you are both very right and very wrong. I hope a year will allow emotions to cool. I think we have to look beyond surface appearances here. I understand that many of you here will think that justice hasn't been served. I know I am opening the law to the possibility of abuse. But, what is it they say, 'A man's gotta do what a man's gotta do.'"

"What kind of sentence would you be passing if my daughter had died?" Delbert James ask.

The judge pause for a long time.

"That's a hypothetical question. I can't answer it."

Delbert James and the judge exchange a long look.

The Porcupine Man

Something bad is gonna happen if this heat don't break soon," Etta said as she smeared me and Frank with the oily goo that kept mosquitoes and black flies at a proper distance.

It was the summer we turned twelve. Everything was sharp and dry that summer. The heat never let up, which was strange for Alberta where the joke is that there are nine months of snow and three months of poor sledding, and where jokes are always closer to the truth than we imagine. The wild roses were thin, the edges of their pale pink petals curled, tiny ants speckled their yellow centers. Leaves were few and thorns plentiful. If you stepped too close the thorns grasped your jeans and held on like angry kittens. Drought-inspired mosquitoes were small and mean, their bites hurt more, and there were more of them. Sometimes so many, especially in the evenings, that you breathed them in, and the thrum of them filled the air like a nasty breeze.

From outside Etta's cabin we could smell the mosquito scare that she brewed in an aluminium pot on the back of the stove. Me and my friend Frank Fencepost went by Etta's often that summer. Our families couldn't afford to buy drug store repellent. Because of so many bites the kids on the reserve looked like they had measles, were whiny and bad tempered. On the reserve that summer everyone was whiny and bad tempered.

We thought about some of the bad things that might happen, fires and murders was what first come to mind, but not even Etta would have guessed that old Nate Sixkiller would be involved.

"Nate was a boy about the same time as me," Etta said, right after the weird business started. Me and Frank laughed at that, pointing out that Etta wasn't a boy. But, guess the heat was even getting to her, for she glare at us until we shut up. We don't want to be on the bad side of Etta, and, as Frank quick to point out, Etta got a bigger bad side than anyone on the reserve. Because Etta don't have any children of her own, me and Frank a few of our friends drink gallons of Kool-Ade that Etta mix in a water bucket on her table, and Etta always have a bandage, a cool cloth, or a cookie, whenever one was badly needed.

If what Etta said was true, and Etta don't lie unless she dealing with government or police, or it is for someone's own good, then Nate Sixkiller must be really old. "Etta was gray-haired when I was a young girl," my ma, Suzie Ermineskin, said more than once. "Etta's old as the hills."

The trouble began way back when Mrs. Zinnia Pelt got mixed up with Pastor Orkin of the Three Seeds of the Spirit, Predestinarian, Bittern Lake Baptist Church.

"Pastor Orkin," Frank says, "has got a black belt in theology."

Mrs. Zinnia Pelt was a Talltree before she married, and she have sisters named Pansy and Marigold, all named for the pictures on seed packages. It only in recent years that Pastor Orkin, who I'm pretty sure he ordained himself, or at the most order up a five dollar certificate from the back of an outdoors magazine with ads for cuckoo clocks, how to make a million stuffing envelopes, learn taxidermy by mail and T-shirts that say "I won't give up my gun until I'm stone cold dead", give up his job in the accounts department for the John Deere Tractor Company and spend his full time preaching. Back when all this stuff happen he was just a wild-eyed weekend evangelist, preach to any two people he might find, even if he was one of the two. Pastor Orkin never made any bones about not liking Indians. I listened to him preach on a street corner in Wetaskiwin, and he point out me and my sister Minnie, when we were just little kids sitting on the grassy boulevard sharing a Popsicle, as examples of people who been punished by God by being born with dark skin.

"Zinnia always been a little more than a brick short of a load," is the way Etta describe her. Her being short on smarts and long on gullible don't surprise me or Etta, for those are the kind of people too often get involved with weird religions.

The story Etta tell is that Mrs. Pelt wander up to one of Pastor Orkin's street corner preachings, come upon him while he is in full rant. She's had a few beers in the Alice Hotel bar and she get caught up in the rhythm of Pastor Orkin's voice and the tambourines being shaken by the pastor's wife and children. Mrs. Pelt start in to dance, and pretty soon she singing in Cree, which Pastor Orkin mistake for a speaking in tongues, something that the lunatic fringe of Christianity does regularly. Some Sundays me and Frank and our girlfriends check on who is serving the biggest potluck lunch, then troop into the church for the last fifteen minutes of the service and the first half hour of the eating. In some of these places half the congregation gobble like turkeys anxious to be fed, then the pastor translate so everyone including the gobblers supposed to understand.

Pastor Orkin was so short of converts that he change his policy on the spot, not only towards Indians, so's Mrs. Zinnia Pelt can belong to his church, but also, temporarily, toward dancing. Pastor Orkin been known to say that a dancing foot and a praying knee can't coexist on the same leg.

Funny thing is that when Mrs. Pelt sober up she stays in Pastor Orkin's clutches. Turn out she is the kind of convert every two-bit evangelist is praying for. She is stupid enough to be sincere, and she don't know no better than to be tenacious.

"She's like one of them ratty little dogs, grip a cuff and don't let go unless you was to bash it with a brick," was how Etta describe her.

"Just like Jehovah's Witnesses," says my mother, Suzie Ermineskin. There are stories we could tell of these mean-looking people, usually women with their hair pulled back until their eyes bulge, trailing a couple of zombie-like children, who try to force their religion on everyone they meet.

After being converted by Pastor Orkin Mrs. Pelt became real interested in this business of speaking in tongues. It was her who first took an interest in Nate Sixkiller.

This is how Etta describe Nate Sixkiller. "He always been slow. Never had two words to say to anybody. As the years pass he move further and further back into the bush, lose his acquaintance with water and soap altogether, live more and more like an animal. He built a little rectangle of a house with a slant roof, one door, one window, the door is so low only a child could enter standing up. The window always covered with thick plastic to keep out the cold in winter and heat in summer. He visit town less and less, then only to trade his government money for sugar, tea, flour and tobacco. Otherwise he live off his trapline, take a few bony whitefish out of Jump Off Joe Creek, snare a few rabbits, catch partridge in seed traps."

A seed trap is a wooden box turned upside down with a slot in one end, covered by a light piece of wood bigger than the slot. The bird pecks at a trail of seed lead up to the door slot. The cover of the slot is an inch or so above ground, and made of that light wood. The bird can see the trail continues so it pecks away and don't even notice it's pushing the slot-covering up. Once the bird is all the way inside, the slot cover slams shut and the bird is forever trapped in the box.

Personally, I only seen Nate Sixkiller once. He was coming out of Ben Stonebreaker's General Store with a heavy looking gunny sack over his shoulder. He was stooped over by age, wearing baggy overalls and a ragged plaid shirt. His hair was slush-gray, long and greasy; his face looked greasy, too, and have nasty-looking red pimples on it. His eyes, in the second he glanced at me, were wild as an animal's. He said something, the tone sound unfriendly to me. I only understand Cree and English. What he said wasn't either.

Maybe Nate said something to her as he was coming out of Ben Stonebreaker's Store, or they passed on the road, or maybe she just heard a rumor about Nate and decided someone that strange and lonely might be a candidate for religious conversion. Because us Indians are considered easy to convert, religious peoples mistake us not saying anything for agreement. We collectively have a lot of experience with the lunatic fringe. What Mrs. Zinnia Pelt was doing way back across the blueberry muskeg near to an overgrown slough, that some people refer to as Lily Lake, was anyone's guess. She follow what look almost like a path leading into the forest and when she follow it for a mile or so she come upon Nate Sixkiller's shack, and Nate Sixkiller himself standing next to a sand cherry bush, groaning and swaying to music only he could hear, singing out in an unknown language.

I was with Etta when Mrs. Zinnia Pelt come bustling back to Hobbema, her skirt full of brambles, twigs in her hair, and hustles into Etta's cabin moving so fast it like she was motor powered.

"Old Nate is speaking one of the mysterious tongues of the Lost Tribes," she proclaim to Etta. "If only Pastor Orkin could hear him, I know he could translate his speech and interpret the blessed message from God that Nate is bringing to mankind."

"Hmmmph," says Etta, which translate loosely as 'Here's a quarter, call someone who cares,' pour Mrs. Pelt a cup of tea from the big brown tea pot squat like a broody hen on Etta's kitchen counter.

"Old Nate's been crazy for more years than you been born," Etta say. "Nate Sixkiller wouldn't know your God from a jack fish."

Mrs. Pelt ain't about to be discouraged. "God works in mysterious ways his wonders to perform," she said, speaking it as if she'd invented the words. After she leave Etta's cabin, she hitch a ride to Wetaskiwin with a rodeo cowboy pulling a horse trailer behind his pickup truck, turn up on Pastor Orkin's doorstep with the news she's found someone genuinely speaking in tongues.

Later on, after he viewed Nate Sixkiller himself, Pastor Orkin would say, "We have discovered, alone in the orchard of the Lord, a man who is pure of heart, and who speaks God's truth."

When the weather was nice enough for outdoor preaching, Pastor Orkin and his family would hang out on various street corners in Wetaskiwin. The pastor, even back then, was a stocky man with a red face, always wear a shiny blue suit glint different colors as he standing under a streetlight. His straight blond hair look like it been cut with a bowl by Mrs. Orkin, a slight-built woman with pale hair in a bun, pastel clothes, ugly brown shoes with square heels, and an overbite. They have two daughters they drag everywhere, girls with pigtails, buck teeth, and high pitched singing voices. Each of the daughters, who about eight and ten, have a recorder, and at a signal from Mrs. Pastor Orkin, they blow a note then launch into a duet of "Let the Sunshine In", or "The Old Rugged Cross".

"Child abuse, pure and simple," My Ma called it, "those poor little girls on the street after the bars close Saturday nights, making fools of themselves like that."

Even now that we grown up, Frank and me, Rufus Firstrider and Robert Coyote, and sometimes our girlfriends, saunter on by the Orkins, and if there is a quiet moment between the singing and preaching, we sing, "Open up your fly and let the sunshine in," then we all shriek like maniacs and run off down the street, while Pastor Orkin point a fat red finger at us and shout, "Blasphemous heathens!" The Orkin daughters are teenagers now, stoop-shouldered and obedient. One of them is married to a frightened-looking boy with a thick neck and fervent eyes, who strums a guitar with his stubby fingers, and hums along with the hymn singing.

Pastor Orkin is pretty skeptical about an old Indian speaking in tongues and proclaiming God's own truth, but he and his family drive to the reserve, follow Mrs. Zinnia Pelt into the woods on a hot, dry afternoon. At that time his congregation consist of a couple of old ladies, the maiden sisters of a bootlegger named Billygoat Barnes, the women who built a church for Pastor Orkin on the shore of Bittern Lake, and six or eight other people Pastor Orkin corralled through his street corner preaching or by proselytizing at the John Deere Plant where he works days in the accounts payable department. I feel sorry for the family, Mrs. Orkin and the girls all with bare arms and legs in the black fly and mosquito-laden air, because Pastor Orkin's religion forbid women to wear blue jeans, or to cut their hair, wear make-up, dance, or do anything their men don't tell them to do.

What convinced Pastor Orkin that he had a true prophet on his hands was seeing Nate Sixkiller handling a porcupine. Most everybody is afraid of porcupines, even though Etta says they don't actually throw their quills, but that porcupines bump into their enemies and swat them with their tails, and their quills sink in and are like fish hooks, real painful to pull out.

What Pastor Orkin, his family, the few members of his congregation, and Mrs. Zinnia Pelt actually see is Nate Sixkiller taking a porcupine out of his seed trap. Nate ain't trying to catch porcupines, though some people, rather than go hungry, and maybe Nate fall into that group, are known to eat them, saying they taste like chicken. But I've heard people say frog legs taste like chicken, and that is a plain lie. The shaking of the tambourines, the soft urgency of the drum as Mrs. Zinnia Pelt lead Pastor Orkin and the dozen or so people down the path from Blue Quills Hall toward where Nate Sixkiller have his shack, make my blood tingle. Pastor Orkin and his friends would deny they are in any way dancing, because they consider dancing sinful, but they really are.

A bunch of us kids been watching, some of us follow along for a while, the path to Nate's place is narrow to start with, get narrower as it get deeper into the wilderness, with rose bushes grasping in the sunny areas, and some dark, ferny fronds swiping at ankles in the foresty areas. There are bluebells and wild asters growing in shady spots, some tiger lilies and Indian paintbrush on sunny knolls, all smaller and more sun-scorched than usual. Most of the kids lose interest and turn around after a quarter mile or so, but me and Sandra Coyote keep on. I only notice now that Sandra been keeping close to me all morning. She is a year younger than me, and wearing a green and white T-shirt with circular stripes. Her hair that is long enough to touch her shoulders, ain't been combed today. Her two front teeth are big as dice, kind of like my own. Sandra's mouth is always open a bit, and her lower lip red and full. Whenever I look at her Sandra smile up at me.

As we walk along I do something I've never done before and reach over and take Sandra's hand. The shock is like I been poked with an electric cattle prod. My hand and arm feel like they are full of needles. We drop to the back of the line and stop under the shade of a couple of spruce trees, the ground is moist and covered in brown needles. We don't actually kiss, just push our mouths together, Sandra's eyes are wide and a deep chocolate brown. I put my arms around her and she leans her head against my shoulder and the warmth of her is so thrilling I don't know any way of expressing what I feel. That was my first kiss and I guess hers too. We do that a couple more times and get pretty good at it before we run and catch up with the procession. Sandra Coyote and me was always friends after that day. Never sweethearts, though she grew into a beautiful girl. When Sandra was seventeen she was shot dead by a jealous boyfriend.

We seen Nate handling the porcupine. By the time Sandra and me caught up with the group at Nate's farm the business was already going on. I'd guess that they found Nate out in the yard. Afterward, Mrs. Zinnia Pelt confirm that they did. He spoke in tongues to them soon as they arrived. Though only Mrs. Pelt knew he wasn't Cree-speaking.

"Praise the Lord," Pastor Orkin was shouting as we approached, and though they echoed him, some of the congregation was already drawing back from the circle they'd formed around Nate and the seed trap in his yard. His log cabin was settling into the earth, weeds growing on the slant roof, there was a lean-to hen house made of chicken wire and slats. A couple of dogs sniffed, whined, and growled. The yard smelled foul as most farm yards do. And if possible, Nate smelled worse than the farm yard. He had obviously peed his pants and worse, and his lack of acquaintance with soap during the long dry spell made for a bad situation.

Mrs. Pelt told Etta later that Nate paid no attention to them. "It was as if we weren't there at all. He got down on his knees, which greatly excited Pastor Orkin, then Nate reached his hand deep into the seed trap, groping for the partridge, prairie chicken, or pheasant he hoped would be there. He just got a grip on the porcupine and pulled it out of the trap."

"I expect Nate was no stranger to getting porcupines in his seed trap," said Etta when I told her the story, but she just listened to Mrs. Pelt. "You get further talking to a concrete wall than trying to talk sense to a religious nut," says Etta. "I'm told if you punch a porcupine straight on the nose you knock it unconscious. I'm guessing that's what Nate did."

"It was a miracle. He pulled the porcupine out, held it up, looked at it, then tossed it into the tall grass next to his cabin," Mrs. Pelt said. "After that Nate sat on the ground, kind of stunned, still mumbling in a language all his own, while Pastor Orkin and his followers knelt in a circle around him and prayed loudly. Then Pastor Orkin said he was going to use his connection with the Almighty to translate Nate Sixkiller's words. And he did. Though what I heard him saying sounded pretty much the same as what Pastor Orkin said whenever he was preaching on a street corner in Wetaskiwin or Camrose. "He's got a lot of gall," Etta said later, "but damn little imagination." He ranted on about believing in Jesus, accepting Jesus, living a life that Jesus would approve of, which meant doing exactly as Pastor Orkin said.

"We have in our midst a prophet of God who will lead us from this wilderness . . . " Pastor Orkin roared, and the people answered with a few Amens and a lot of hallelujahs.

Then Nate fainted, his eyes rolling back in his head, and Pastor Orkin blessed the event as a miracle, for apparently prophets are supposed to both suffer and faint. They waited around until Nate came to and began mumbling again. Then they went off singing hymns, and rejoicing with great fervor, as Pastor Orkin called it, though they were so mosquito-bitten they probably needed blood transfusions.

"Probably fainted from hunger," said Etta.

They were back the next day and took it as a sign, since there was no evidence of the porcupine in the tall grass, that it had been tamed by Nate's faith.

"A true prophet suffers for his followers," Pastor Orkin declared. But being mosquito bit wasn't for Pastor Orkin and his congregation who mostly lived in Wetaskiwin and Camrose. "I hear the Lord commanding me to carry our brother the prophet to a safe place where he may prosper and speak to us again of the miracles the Lord has in store for us."

Old Nate was so sick and uncomfortable he didn't put up any resistance when a couple of men picked him up and carried him down the path toward Blue Quills Hall, which named for a spruce tree, not a porcupine. They had some discussion as to whether a prophet should require, or be given medical treatment.

"If he's a prophet he should be able to cure hisself," one of the congregation said. They finally did take him to the hospital in Wetaskiwin, where a doctor said he was suffering from malnutrition among other things, and filled him up with antibiotics. Pastor Orkin himself took Nate home to recuperate. The Orkins washed Nate down time after time until he was clean and shiny as everything else in the Orkin household. One of Pastor Orkin's new converts was a barber in a tiny town called Gwynne, and he volunteered to cut Nate's hair, and oil it down, and brush talcum powder on the back of his neck so he smelled like a new baby. He cut

Pastor Orkin's hair, too, made him look more like a banker or a car salesman, than a poor clerk masquerading as a man of God. They dressed Nate up in a perfectly good suit that the barber had gotten too fat for, bought him a white shirt at Robinson's Store in Wetaskiwin, fastened his neck with a tie, one with green palm trees painted on it, from Pastor Orkin's own collection. "You can dress a bear up in a suit," says Etta, "but no matter how you look at it all you got is a bear in a suit."

One problem with do-gooders is that they expect to be rewarded for their good deeds. They expect recipients to be grateful. Nate never let on that anything was different, though he did eat big meals provided by the congregation. "He eats like an animal," Mrs. Zinnia Pelt confided to Etta, but then she went on to say that afterwards he more or less rewarded his benefactors by singing into his tea cup for a long time. Though it may never have been said out loud, it was certainly the consensus that a prophet of God would have the good manners to be grateful.

After less than a week of being passed around among the church people, Nate crawled out a window at Pastor Orkin's in the middle of the night, and by morning was back at his sod-roofed hovel on the reserve, his clothes ripped and filthy, his eyes darting rapidly like an animal under attack. Smart people would have considered their experiment a failure and gone on to something else. Unfortunately, religious people have an inbred tenacity about them that defies common sense.

The day they made their last trip to Nate Sixkiller's place, there was a harmonica and accordion playing as they marched. As they go past her cabin Etta turn her good ear in their direction, say to me that the song is called "The St. James Infirmary Blues".

"I don't think it's a religious song," Etta goes on.

There must have been twenty people with Pastor Orkin that day. Mrs. Pelt says there was a lot of new people at their Sunday service, people who heard through the white people's equivalent of the moccasin telegraph that Pastor Orkin found himself a genuine prophet of God.

"A-men, brothers and sisters," shouted Luke Dupuis the harmonica player, the only black man in Wetaskiwin. He play harmonica outside the door at the Canadian Legion Hall some Saturday nights, have his cap on the ground to accept change, otherwise he was a porter on the railroad, come from a far away state called Louisiana. "Where I come from, they is a Pastor Orkin on every street corner," he say.

"How come you know so much?" I asked Etta, after she go on to explain that "The St. James Infirmary Blues" is a jazz song, and where jazz come from and why it can be both sad and happy at the same time.

"When you've lived as long as me, you know everything," she reply, staring at me unblinking, so there is no way I could tell if she was teasing.

What went on back across the blueberry muskeg that day nobody ever gonna know for certain. Everybody who was there have a different version, and about the only thing everybody agree on is that Nate Sixkiller ain't acting the way a prophet of God is expected to. And because of that Pastor

Orkin and some of his congregation was thoroughly upset. The RCMP investigated off and on for six months, must have had a thousand pages of typed up interviews, but they decide nobody will be charged with anything. They don't even know for sure that anything illegal was done.

Most likely Nate died by himself and Pastor Orkin and Company decided to cremate both him and his shack. Or, possibly, Nate locked himself inside and set his own place on fire in order to get away from all the prying religious fanatics. Pastor Orkin had the most to lose if Nate stopped co-operating with him. He already had posters and handbills printed and was planning a revival meeting on the grounds of The Sons of Sweden Hall, not far from Bittern Lake, complete with an outdoor tent for sermonizing, that they'd already signed up to rent from Acme Novelty and Carnival Supplies Store in Edmonton. On the posters there was a drawing on someone being dunked in a lake by a white-gowned preacher, who resembled pastor Orkin.

Somebody said they seen Pastor Orkin lighting the cabin afire with a lighter. Pastor Orkin was quick to deny that but for a different reason that you never would of thought. He said he wouldn't use a lighter because it is an instrument of the Devil, because it is used to light cigarettes, and cigarettes are instruments of the devil as well.

Maybe after everybody left, Nate's cabin was struck by lightning, that don't seem likely, though there were black clouds on the horizon with zippers of lightning and the rumble of thunder that entire day.

"Probably Nate went to sleep with a cigarette in his hands," says Etta, who tends toward the practical.

And that would have been that except for Luke Dupuis. Luke, who got a lazy smile on his face all the time so it's impossible to tell what he's really thinking, tell Pastor Orkin that he got a good thing going for him even if he don't understand it. He go on to tell the pastor about something called snake handling that ministers do all the time in the deep south of the United States where Luke come from. "Too cold up here to have real snakes," Luke go on, "and no point in using little local garter snakes, handling snakes only counts when they're poisonous, preferably deadly."

Pastor Orkin says he don't like snakes, but he's advertized the tent meeting and what with his genuine speaking-in-tongues, porcupine-handling prophet dead and gone he needed something to draw the people in.

"If you got faith," Luke Dupuis say with his ever-present smile, "you'll be able to handle a porcupine, just like Nate, and the presence of the Lord will make it gentle as a lamb, and you'll hold it up to the cheers of the crowd and won't get a single quill in you."

Pastor Orkin send Mrs. Zinnia Pelt to Etta with a rush order for a porcupine. Me and Frank agree to trap a porcupine for ten dollars each. We immediately walk out to Nate Sixkiller's place, and find the seed trap been thrown into the tall grass not far from the cabin. Don't take but a day to trap the porcupine, though it take a lot longer to get it and the trap back to civilization and then into Wetaskiwin. I won't go into details about my own wounds, let's just say Frank was standing at the tent meeting, and intended on standing for another two weeks after the tent meeting.

This is Pastor Orkin's big chance. There are close to 200 people come to the tent meeting, and his porcupine-handling get advertized on posters, and the local radio take an interest because this is such a strange event.

Pastor Orkin work himself into a frenzy, praising the Lord, cursing His enemies, which according to Pastor Orkin is anybody don't believe exactly the way he do. They got the porcupine on a table up on stage in an aquarium with a thick plank over the top. The porcupine rolled itself into a ball and try to pretend nothing unusual is happening.

Pretty soon Pastor Orkin's followers get to speaking in tongues, and members of the audience join right in. Pastor Orkin, as Frank say, "roar like a gored boar," and prance around the stage calling up the power of Jesus.

"Lord, help him tame the fury of the wild beast, and through my faith make it gentle as a baby."

The crowd is really getting into it, everybody on their feet, swaying back and forth, many of them speaking in tongues.

Pastor Orkin take the lid off the aquarium.

A couple of days ago Luke Dupuis was hanging out on the porch of Louis Coyote's General Store, smiling sweetly as always and telling how in the South, the snake handlers over the years get used to being bit.

"The secret of their act is to pick up the snakes and not flinch when they get bit so the audience never know the difference. Over the years they build up a tolerance to snake venom," Luke said. "It's not that they don't get bit, it's that they're good actors."

"What's gonna happen to Pastor Orkin?" we ask. "He ain't got no experience being filled full of porcupine quills."

"Ain't that true?" says Luke Dupuis, smile even more angelically than usual.

The Pastor is out of action for about a month and when he start preaching again all that's left is his family and a couple of slow learners like Mrs. Zinnia Pelt.

Etta, who was the one who waddle up to the stage and rescue Pastor Orkin, say he have to get tetanus, rabies, and goodness knows what all kind of shots for the bites the porcupine inflict on him, after it fill his body full of quills in more places than you would imagine.

Practical People

There aren't very many happy married couples around the reserve, but of the few I've seen, Wayne and Marlene Horse is the happiest. They is the kind of couple don't ordinarily get noticed much. Neither of them ever been in any kind of trouble, they is friendly and polite, keep their house painted, don't drink and stay away from the rowdy people who do. They don't have any enemies I know of. They both work in Wetaskiwin, Wayne as a desk clerk at the Travelodge Motel, while Marlene is a nurses' helper at the Sundance Retirement Home.

Wayne is twenty-four years old, Marlene a year or two younger. They got a girl toddler name of Leslie, look like a little brown doll you might see in a toy store display, and a baby boy named for Wayne that they call Junior.

Wayne and Marlene Horse are about the most organized couple I know, and I learn a lot from them about handling money. Now, if I just had some money to handle. The Horses have a big, blue-covered account book in which they enter every purchase, no matter how small. At the top of each column is an amount, and when that amount been spent for the month, they don't spend no more.

"This way we know where every penny goes. If we're spending too much money on say, entertainment, then we stop renting videos or going to movies and concerts until we can afford it."

"We use our credit cards to actually save money," Marlene chimes in. "We buy something on sale, don't get billed for a month. After the bill comes there are two or three more weeks before we have to pay, all that while our money is in the bank earning interest."

"We're practical people," Wayne say. "Except for our mortgage, we've never, ever paid a penny in interest," he say proudly.

"What do you file condoms under?" Frank ask, peering over Wayne's shoulder into the account book. "Entertainment? Necessities? Sports?"

"Pharmaceuticals," says Wayne, as if Frank asked a serious question. Wayne is a guy who when they passed out a sense of humor, was studying his bookkeeping.

"Actually, we didn't practise any birth control until after our second child was born. We agreed that two was a sufficient family. Consequently, I had a vasectomy, paid for by medical insurance."

"I just remembered," say Frank, "it's time for me to go slam my hand in the car door."

Wayne stare at him curiously through his thick glasses, but don't crack a smile.

Guess they might have spent their whole lives being happy and unnoticed if Wayne hadn't took sick.

It was me who drove Wayne up to the doctor's office in Wetaskiwin on a sunny August afternoon. He been off work for three or four days, say he feel weak and want to sleep all the time, have spots in front of his eyes sometimes. Because of the spots I drove him in his car, a Plymouth two-door hatchback, painted a kind of road color, have a standard transmission, and not even a radio. "We bought it after the next year's models come out," Wayne tell me, which by now don't surprise me. He list about ten more reasons the car was a bargain, it being a demonstrator and model that was being discontinued were at the head of the list.

I remember when they bought the car, me and my friends was scanning the car lot in Wetaskiwin, playing wish book, when we see they is serious about this dull looking demonstrator car. We try to talk them into getting a new, bright colored car with racing stripes and shiny wheel covers. Wayne has already test drove this one three times, and taken it to Fred Crier's garage in Hobbema for an examination.

"At least get a tape deck that plays CDs," we plead.

"We don't spend money on CDs," Wayne says. "The radio plays everything we want to hear and for free. We don't even need a radio in the car because we have one at home."

"How about a sun roof," says Frank.

"Just something else to go wrong," says Wayne. Sun roofs spring leaks in the summer and let heat escape in the winter. A car is simply a means of getting from point A to point B."

"I prefer getting from point A to point B at about a hundred miles an hour, with a tape deck booming, and pretty girl reclining on the plush upholstery next to me, while she performing an amateur medical examination and providing an available treatment for what ails me," say Frank.

Wayne don't even smile, just try to convince the salesman to lower the price twenty more dollars because of a new scratch he found on the back fender.

The reason Wayne and I become friends is because of astronomy.

"I've never been more than a hundred miles from the reserve in my life, but by studying the stars and planets I've seen the whole universe," Wayne tell me one time while I'm visiting with him at the Travelodge. "Tomorrow's my day off and my mother-in-law is going to babysit so Marlene and I can go to the planetarium in Edmonton. Would you like to come with us?"

I went with them. Wayne talk astronomy all the way there, and it don't seem like there is a lot he don't know. Most all of it go in one ear and out the other, I don't think it even go in my ear, times when Wayne start naming off the craters on the moon, that information sort of veer right around me, though I remember there was one named Werner, which sound to me like a German Shepherd dog.

I don't get a whole lot more out of the show at the planetarium. We are inside in a theater, but it give the impression we're sitting on a hillside staring up at the night sky.

Astronomy never been one of my interests, I couldn't even name but two or three planets, even if you was to pay me ten dollars a piece. At the planetarium they lecture about asteroids, comets, double and multiple stars, and stars that orbit each other. Then there are nebulae, and galaxies, and constellations.

The sky is sure nice to look at but about all I remember is there's a constellation called Gemini, which is my birth sign. They showed it on the screen but I couldn't pick out the shape of the twins. Frank claim his sign is Sanitary Landfill Two Miles.

I can see where you could spend a lifetime with astronomy as a hobby. Wayne talked all the way back to Wetaskiwin of white dwarfs, visual binaries, and a star called Sirius that really named for a dog. That evening he took me up on the roof of the Travelodge and let me look through his binoculars. I was able to spot Orion, the Seven Sisters, and quite a few other planets and constellations, after Wayne set them up for me.

To be honest I would rather have been reading a book, but I try to be polite and pretend I'm enjoying myself, though there is a frost-carrying wind coming down off the Rocky Mountains, and up on that roof I'm shivering like a last leaf in my light jacket, while Wayne's face is glowing in the moonlight like he is lit up from the inside.

"I'm saving for a real good telescope," Wayne tell me. "A quality one is expensive." And when he tell me how much, it is about seven times more than I would have ever guessed. "Trouble is we're saving for a word processor and programs to help Marlene study nursing. Both those things are a couple of years down the line, though we set aside a predetermined percentage of our monthly income."

Yes, they are practical people alright.

"I'm glad I've always understood my duty toward my family," Wayne say to me as we driving back toward Hobbema, after we been to the doctor.

Wayne tell me they took about twenty blood samples at the lab around the corner from the doctor's office, and that the doctor look real worried when Wayne describe his symptoms.

"I'm afraid I might have something serious," he say, "and the doctor didn't deny it, just told me to hope for the best and come back day after tomorrow to look at the test results."

I have to ask a couple more questions before I learn that what he mean by 'duty toward his family' is life insurance.

"Because I've studied financial planning, I carry $200,000 worth of term insurance on my life, and I added another $100,000 after each child. If I die Marlene and the babies won't suffer financially."

"I guess not," I say.

I wonder if it is because he studied accounting and financial planning that make Wayne talk like a message on an answering machine.

That total is more money than I figure existed.

"You probably got nothing worse than the flu," I say.

But Wayne do have something a lot worse than the flu. When his tests are ready he is still too sick to drive. It is something called galloping leukemia, have to do with one set of red dots in his blood is eating up a set of white dots, or maybe the other way round, Wayne explains to me on the drive back to the reserve. He stopped at a bookstore and bought a book called *Living with Leukemia*, which he is crouched forward in the passenger seat studying as we drive.

"What account you figure you'll charge that book to?"

Serious as always, Wayne calculate for a minute. It never occur to him that I'm teasing so to make him forget his troubles.

I've just told him the story about the thief who don't understand procedures too well. "So this guy got arrested for knocking a woman down and snatching her purse," I say. "They put him in a police line-up with five other guys. When the victim walk into the room, the thief look her up and down, point at her and say, 'That's her.'"

Instead of at least snickering when I finish the story, Wayne say, "He should have retained a good lawyer."

What do you do with a guy like that?

"I'll have to consult with Marlene, but I think Education," is the way Wayne answer about the book. "It could go under entertainment though, or maybe medical."

"I'd vote for medical," I say, treating the subject as seriously as he does.

I get to drive Wayne to the doctor's office quite a few more times. They put him on chemotherapy right away and it seem his appointments always coincide with Marlene's working hours.

Pointing out for the umpteenth time that he and Marlene are practical people, Wayne say he won't let the doctors play any games with him. Him and Marlene sit down with them and Wayne have a tape recorder along so he can listen to the replies to all his questions as many times as he likes.

"I have a particularly pernicious strain of leukemia," he tells me. "From their experience the doctors say I've got about three months to live. Four or five if I'm real lucky. All I can hope for is a remission, and that hardly ever happens with this kind."

He go on to tell me he's transferred all his assets to Marlene. "I don't even exist any more. If someone was to look me up in a computer they wouldn't find me. I turned in my driver's license, got a five dollar refund coming. Every dollar counts." I wait for him to laugh, but he don't. "I sold my hockey card collection to an outfit in Edmonton. I could have left them for Wayne Jr. but what if he has no interest in them and just played with them?"

"You taken your clothes to the Goodwill yet?" I ask.

"Marlene will take care of that as soon as I'm gone. I've arranged to be cremated, so Marlene can sell both my suits. I bargained the undertaker down to under five hundred dollars for the whole thing. I have a burial policy with the Elk's Lodge that pays a thousand dollars no questions asked, a little more for Marlene to put aside."

"I suppose you got a VCR box put aside for your ashes so Marlene won't have to buy an urn." I figure this has got to raise a smile.

"Certainly," says Wayne, "providing my own container for my ashes was one of my bargaining points."

Practical people. But honest. Wayne calculate the distance to the doctor's office in Wetaskiwin, and later to a specialist in Edmonton, calculate it in kilometers instead of real measurements like miles, so I have to trust him. He works out some kind of formula taking into consideration that I'm driving his car. Then he offer me one lump sum for driving him until he either dies or his leukemia goes into remission. "If it goes into remission we'll renegotiate." It take me a while with my kid sister Delores' calculator, but I figure Wayne saving three dollars a trip by offering a lump sum, but if he lives over four months he saves a whole lot more.

"What you got there?" I ask Marlene Horse, as I lean in the window of her car which is parked on the main street of

Wetaskiwin. The whole passenger seat is filled with one squat box, while a long thin one run from the windshield overtop the seat, and nearly to the back window. A month has passed and I visit Wayne almost every day, drive him to his appointments. He is pale and losing weight. I found a video about astronomy at West Edmonton Mall. It wasn't for rent, only for sale. At the store I tried to think like Wayne. Instead of paying $29.95 for the video, I offered to leave thirty dollars with the clerk, bring the video back the next day, and let him keep five dollars for his trouble. He accepted my offer and never batted an eye. Wayne really enjoy the video, and he even smiled when I told him how I acquired it.

"Something for Wayne," is the way Marlene answers my question.

"Let's see," I say. "I bet there's a gun in the long box and ammunition in the small one." I decide that was a really stupid thing for me to say, so I try to cover up. It wouldn't surprise me if Wayne would consider killing himself to save a few bucks. "Or, maybe you got Wayne a set of mops, and the small box is full of cleaning supplies? How about curtain rods and curtains?"

"It's a telescope," Marlene says with not even a trace of a smile.

"I bet he'll like that," I say.

"I bought it."

"I bet he won't like that."

But he does like it. He calculates that Marlene will be able to sell it for about seventy-five percent of what she paid. "Sometimes an emotional gesture takes precedence over financial economy," says Wayne.

"I want him to see where he's going," Marlene says, looking at Wayne with so much love it kind of make me shiver.

While Frank and me hanging out at Ben Stonebreaker's Store, sitting in the sun on the wide front porch, me drinking diet soda, Frank drinking something called Jolt that have twice as much sugar and caffeine as ordinary soda, Wayne come down the street, walking bent over like an old man, his wine-colored sweater hanging baggy over his thin body. Even though Wayne and Marlene live only about three blocks away he is breathing heavy and shaking by the time he climb the steps to the store.

"I hate to ask for a favor," says Wayne, "but could you guys come over this evening. It's supposed to be clear and there's some stars I'd like to see. Marlene has to work and I need help with the stairs, and moving the telescope."

"No problem," I tell him. I have to kick Frank so he agree too.

After Wayne leaves, we go inside and Frank with his pupils dilated and kind of a silly grin on his face buy another bottle of Jolt. We notice that Ben Stonebreaker got two shelves of nothing but oatmeal this week.

"You must sell a lot of oatmeal," says Frank.

Ben, standing behind the counter wearing his red baseball cap with the long bill, adjust the collar of his denim jacket, pull on one of his long white braids like he often does.

"Actually, I don't," he says. He smile his soft, brown smile. "But the salesman who stock my shelves, he sells a lot of oatmeal."

"I think I'm gonna find me a place right about on Orion's belt, that's where I'll set up and keep an eye on everybody. So you guys better behave yourselves," says Wayne.

"I've evaded scrutiny by better men than you," says Frank, going along with the joke.

"I bet you're gonna go into remission any day now," I say. "You'll probably be around ten years from now."

"I'm resigned," said Wayne.

"It all depends how you look at it," says Frank. "Resigned, and re-signed are about the same word, but one's positive and one's negative. I think I'll do a sermon on that for Brother Frank's Gospel Hour. Maybe you could come on the show, Wayne, and we'll pray over you and come up with a miracle cure. It's easy to do on the radio. I'll have you throw away your crutches. Easy to do with sound effects. A lot harder to do in person."

"I'm not using crutches, yet," Wayne point out. "I'm way beyond this religious foolishness. I'm part of nature, I'm going back to nature, everybody does, I just have a little shorter lifespan than some."

That night, after we poke the telescope out Wayne's up-stairs window we look close up at at the Seven Sisters, which up close is more like ten or eleven, Orion, the Big and Little Dipper, and lots of constellations Wayne point out but whose names don't stick with me.

"I wonder about this telescope," Wayne says. "I'd almost like for Marlene to keep it, that way she could more or less keep in touch with me. But Marlene doesn't get excited about astronomy, and my kids are too little, though I hope at least one of them will enjoy a telescope later on. That's the only thing I've asked Marlene to promise me, that she'll introduce the kids to astronomy when they get older. The thing that breaks my heart about dying is leaving Marlene and the kids."

"I've had my eye on that stethoscope," say Frank, a day or two after Wayne's funeral. "I figure there's more than one kind of heavenly body I could watch with something that powerful."

Frank figure he could place the telescope somewhere get a close-up of the dressing room at Blue Quills Hall where Molly Thunder's dance troupe, the Duck Lake Massacre, change clothes before and after rehearsal.

"My sister, Delores is in that troupe," I say, glaring at Frank.

"Hey, once we get set up I'll give you first peek. You tell me which one is your sister and I won't look at her."

When we get to Marlene's she is busy loading the car with stuff, got both passengers doors wide open and the trunk lid up. I can see the stand for the telescope already peeking out of the back end, and Marlene is coming down the sidewalk, dressed in jeans and a wine-colored parka, carrying the telescope.

"I figured I might buy that telescope from you," I say to Marlene. "Watching the universe with Wayne made me aware of some thing I never thought about . . . "

"He wants to shoot some intergalactic beaver," says Frank. "Personally, I want to spot that star ship Enterprise. Couple of time I been where no man has been before, but if I could get them to beam me up . . . "

Marlene lay the telescope on a folded blanket in the trunk. As she turn around to me she say, "Silas, do you think it's okay to lie to someone when the lie makes them feel good?"

"Most times," I say.

"I lied to Wayne."

"About what?"

"The telescope."

"How do you mean?"

"It ain't for sale."

"How come?"

"I don't own it."

"But, you said . . . "

"I didn't want to lose the interest on our savings. Or take a loss. I rented the telescope for sixty days." Practical people.

Threes

T hings oftentimes come in threes," our medicine lady, Mad
Etta say. Etta is usually right. Take last summer. There was
this white man who live on the reserve that we Indians
wanted to get rid of, while at the same time there was a
different white man that we wanted to keep. And then there
was an Indian woman who the powers that be wanted to get
rid of. Sounds complicated and it was. How those three events
all joined together is the story I want to tell.

Gus Munro was the guy we wanted to get rid of. He is
white and been living on the reserve for years with an Indian
lady name of Sadie Horseshoe. He been here so long he not
only consider himself an Indian, he forget entirely that he
is white. He call himself Gus Muskeg, and so do we. Even
get his mail by that name down to Ben Stonebreaker's Store.
Gus is a short man with a barrel chest, sleepy brown eyes
and a sagging face like an old dog. He is maybe fifty, and
speak pretty fair Cree, but talk both English and Cree with
an accent he think sound like the rest of us. While we still
liked him nobody was rude enough to tell him any different.

The guy we want to keep on the reserve (I just read somewhere that some white-Indian in Ontario or Quebec, for whatever reason, want to have reserves referred to as *territories*. I prefer to see things the way Etta does. "It don't matter what you call a skunk, it still smell skunky.") is Einar Valgardson, who comes from a place called Iceland, that is forever north of us, and even colder than Alberta. He is built like one of those super heroes in comic books, tall with muscles bulge all over him, long blond hair and eyes blue as moonlight.

Einar just walk onto the reserve one day, say in his heavy-accented English that he traveling around the world, and he would like to live with some Indians for a while. He had money to buy board and room so we moved him in with Mrs. Francine Fencepost, Frank's mother. He is a real talker, and after a while we can understand everything he say to us, he tell us lots of stories about Iceland, but he is the same kind of storyteller as me, it really difficult to tell what might be truth and what might be fiction.

The only bad thing is that Einar, being a big, handsome white guy, have the local girls falling all over him like he was made of candy. That mean there are a few Indian guys with their noses out of joint, because their girlfriends, or would-be girlfriends, hang all over Einar Valgardson. It funny, but some girls who never get a second glance from local boys, become real desirable soon as Einar Valgardson give them a hug down at Hobbema Pool Hall. Other girls manage to get lots of attention from their boyfriends by letting them know if Einar was to look at them they'd be in his bed in a flash.

By the time we find out Einar Valgardson ain't quite who he seem to be, there was enough people liked him that we hide him so the RCMP can't carry him off to jail.

The woman who is supposed to be evicted from the reserve is Eva McCarty. She was born Eva Springwater, and when she was about eighteen she run off and marry a guy named Don McCarty who was oil field worker she met in the Alice Hotel beer parlor. They live in a house trailer out around Violet Grove for a year or two, then when the oil field work dry up they move to Nova Scotia, where McCarty's home town is. We don't figure to hear from Eva again. And ten years pass before we do. She turn up on her mother's doorstep, have a boy and a girl in tow. The boy is about eight, have blond hair like his daddy, with Eva's dark skin, and his own dust-colored eyes. The little girl look to be all Indian, round faced, blackeyed, have her hair tied in little braids with red ribbon on each end. Her name is Annie and she is so cute everybody want to hug her.

Eva had got a divorce mainly because her husband was drunk all the time; she live in Toronto for a year or so before coming home. She only been at her mother's for a few weeks when Samantha Yellowknees, Chief Tom Crow-eye's girlfriend, get wind of her being there. Samantha actually come out to the reserve, snoop around asking questions.

Chief Tom and Samantha live in an apartment in Wetaskiwin. She is an Ontario Indian and they would both like to be white if they could, not have to associate with us regular Indians anymore.

What Samantha discover, by reading some of the forty or so volumes of memos and instructions get issued from Ottawa by the department of Indian Affairs, is that once an Indian woman marries a white man, she lose her status as an Indian, forever.

"You mean by saying 'I do', I can become a white man?" my friend Frank Fencepost say. "Boy, I'm gonna marry me three or four white women just in case it don't take the first time."

"Don't work that way," says Bedelia Coyote, our resident thorn in the side of the government, who spend her life trying to undo all the sneaky things Chief Tom, Samantha and the rest of the governments try to pull. "Only Indian women lose out when they marry a white man. You," she glare at Frank like if he was a pincushion he'd be full of pins, "could marry a dozen white women and the government would give them all the benefits of being an Indian. But, an Indian woman who marries outside the tribe become invisible, a nothing. She's still an Indian, but the government says she's white, or at least not an Indian no more."

Nothing stop Samantha Yellowknees.

"What are you afraid Eva gonna do?" we ask Samantha, "drink too much well water, pick too many berries, crush the grass by walking on it? Why don't you just leave her well enough alone?"

"One of the chief's jobs is to enforce the Indian Act. Eva McCarty and her children have no right to live on the reserve. They are a financial burden. We intend to relieve the reserve of that burden."

"Chief Tom is gutless as a cleaned fish," says Bedelia.

"If you was ever to marry Chief Tom, you'd lose your status," says Frank.

"Ain't nobody ever told you," I say, "Chief Tom ain't been an Indian for must be going on ten years. He got himself declared white by a law court. Didn't you know?"

By this time Samantha caught on to the joke.

Because of Samantha, Eva get a letter with about five dollars worth of stamps on it, tell her on Department of Indian Affairs writing paper that she have thirty days for her and her kids to leave the reserve.

The reason we want to get rid of Gus Muskeg, don't have anything to do with him being white, it is because he turned militant on us. That may sound strange, because white people tend to think all Indians always agree with each other. That certainly ain't the truth.

There is some tribal business too complicated to explain, or for most people to understand. What happen is Gus Muskeg get real involved in local politics, though he can't even vote he bring his wife along to vote for him. We are quiet-living people, and Gus Muskeg, even though he campaigning for what he think is best for all us Indians, have a loud voice, irritate a lot of people, until we consider him more of a nuisance than a help.

Gus get some friends on his side and they feel they been short changed when it come to getting their hands on government grant money. They think, and rightly so, that Chief Tom, Samantha and company, only distribute what they have to and only to people who do them favors. The more noisy him and his group get the less money they see.

"What Gus Munro and his friends don't understand," Bedelia Coyote say, "is something that it's taken me a few years to learn, in politics you reward your friends and punish your enemies. That's the way it is and will always be."

Bedelia used to kick walls and cuss like a rodeo cowboy, whenever the bureaucracy put one over on her, which was most of the time. But she's learned to deal with them. She just read the fine print closer and a couple more times than anybody else. Last year she filled out about a half ton of forms, made me sign my name in a few places, send them off to Ottawa. In a few months I get a letter in a big, brown envelope, signed by the Deputy Minister of some department or other, that say I been approved to give a reading of my work at Blue Quills Hall, right here in Hobbema, on a certain night, and that I'll be paid $1200 in cash, plus mileage (35 cents a kilometer) to get there if I need it, and a night at a hotel if I need that, too.

I measure it off and figure that it's about 300 yards from my cabin to Blue Quills Hall. "I reckon I could charge about 8 cents for transportation," I tell Bedelia, "trouble is it would cost five times that to mail in the form. What I'd really like is for me and Sadie to spend a night at the Travelodge Motel in Wetaskiwin."

"Spend two," says Bedelia. "If you'd read any of those forms you'd know that I'm your sponsor, or at least The Tamarack Ecological Arts Co-op and Reading Series is, that's a name I made up to impress the government. I'll okay two nights in the motel, and meals, but you got to donate $400 to the Arts Co-op. That's how Chief Tom and Samantha do it. I've learned over the years that I can't beat them, though I never stop trying, but I'm gonna more-or-less join them. If you're honest with them you end up losing. The government expect people to be dishonest, you just have to learn how far you can go without triggering an investigation."

But Gus Munro and his friends ain't learned that lesson yet. Gus lead a group of five or six friends, and they occupy the offices on the reserve, disrupt things even more than they already are. They call their group Fair Share. They plunk themselves down in the band offices, armed with food and sleeping bags, make the staff work around them until quitting time. Then they sing songs for a while, pass the peace pipe, spread out sleeping bags on the floor. Gus sleep on Chief Tom's fancy oak desk with the glass cover, while Sadie

Horseshoe and their kids set up a TV and pass around packages of Fritos.

Chief Tom usually keep his cool; he let Samantha Yellowknees get angry for him. "He ain't smart enough to get mad," is how Frank Fencepost describe him. But, boy, Frank should have been there like I was when Chief Tom arrive the next morning to find all these people in his office eating Egg McMuffins and spilling coffee. What piss him off the most is that Gus Munro (Muskeg) let his sleeping bag slip from under him during the night and his belt buckle, what weigh about three pounds, put a lot of deep scratches on the chief's glass-topped desk.

What bring things to a head is that Bedelia Coyote and her friends are more upset with Gus Munro than Chief Tom and Samantha, if that's possible. While they occupying the office, they get to playing with the shredder Chief Tom acquire to dispose of secret documents, and they shred a ton of stuff, some of it applications and correspondence of Bedelia's, who, having just learned how to milk the system, is enjoying her role as resident shit disturber and don't want any competition.

After negotiations that go all the way to evening, Chief Tom and Samantha, by promising a full investigation into Gus Munro's complaints, get his group to leave the band offices.

Once they are gone, and the place cleaned up, a real meeting commence, with old enemies smiling across the table at each other as they unite to rid themselves of a common nuisance.

"This group, Fair Share, is nothing without Gus Munro," says Samantha Yellowknees. "All we got to do is get rid of him."

Sitting in as Bedelia's assistant, I'm the one who mention that Gus ain't an Indian, something everyone else apparently forgot.

"Of course," says Samantha, "we've been making a simple situation difficult. We simply refuse to discuss anything with Gus; we refuse to attend any meetings where he's present, and if they pull another occupation or demonstration we have the RCMP come in and arrest Gus, but leave everyone else alone."

"And if he keeps on disturbing the status quo," says Chief Tom, "we'll have him evicted from the reserve. After all, he's a white man living on Indian land."

Ordinarily both me and Bedelia would have made some sarcastic remarks at that point, but right now we need Chief Tom and Samantha. Somewhere I read that you got to love your enemies in order to understand them, or maybe it was the other way round.

Over the next few days Chief Tom do whatever is necessary to get a white man who is squatting on Indian land removed from the reserve. The RCMP come out to Sadie Horseshoe's cabin, serve Gus Munro with an order to "quit his illegal abode within fourteen days," or else they will remove him bodily.

As you can imagine Gus don't take kindly to that. He take the eviction paper to a lawyer in Edmonton, one who is known for handling labor disputes, and sure enough he draw up some papers that say exactly opposite of the eviction notice and serve them on Chief Tom and Samantha, and everybody even loosely connected with the administration of the band office. That lawyer is named White and he is the kind of guy that if he is on your side you consider him a hero, but if he's on the other side he is a sleazy little troublemaker. Both definitions apply. Mr. White is an expert at delaying, and over a year has passed and Gus Munro still lives on the reserve, and still makes some trouble, though the provision about him not being able to attend business meetings still applies, and has slowed him down some.

While we are fighting to get rid of Gus Munro we are, ironically, at the same time, fighting to keep this other white man, Einar Valgardson. It is Frank Fencepost who get wind of the fact the RCMP coming to arrest Einar Valgardson. Einar been living on the reserve for maybe six months. Far as I can see what he adds is more than he subtracts. He get thin, purple air mail letters from Iceland, which always contain money, so Einar is more than able to pay his way. He paint the Fencepost's cabin, for the first time in its existence. He build flower boxes under both front windows, and now, in summer, they overflow with geraniums, petunias, and other colorful flowers. Einar realize that all the girls liking him could be a serious problem. If he was Frank he would probably be dead by now, because Frank would take every opportunity presented to him. But, Einar, while letting the girls know that he is flattered by their attention, manage to send them away without hurt feelings. Once the guys see that he ain't really after their women, they decide to accept him as a friend. Einar do settle in on a girl named Ermine LaViolette, someone who lived near me all her life and sort of grew up while I wasn't looking, and turned into a very beautiful girl with long hair and a slim figure, who making a name for herself as a barrel-racer at local rodeos.

This was at a time when Frank was sneaking into the Indian radio station, K-UGH, late at night, and was just starting to broadcast a version of what would later become Brother Frank's Gospel Hour.

The news come in in the middle of the night on the Teletype machine of how the RCMP searching for, and expect to imminently arrest this man from Iceland who is wanted in his own country for being a political terrorist. Back there he organize demonstrations against the government, and lead protesters who fight with police, break windows, damage and occupy government buildings.

"Hey, Iceland man," Frank say into the radio, "we think it's time for you to become a famous potato and go underground," and Frank laugh at his own cleverness.

It is a couple of days before the RCMP come rolling onto the reserve, driving real slow in case we pulled up a culvert as we been known to do. We claim total ignorance. "No big white man with blond hair ever lived on the reserve, not in the past, not in the present, and for sure not in the future," we tell Constable Bobowski, the lady RCMP who, far too slowly, is learning how to work with us Indians.

"But I've seen him, when I've been here on other matters," Constable Bobowski insist. "I've seen him at the pool hall, and even in Wetaskiwin at the Gold Nugget cafe." Constable Bobowski is at the door of Fencepost's cabin. Mrs. Francine Fencepost suddenly forgot how to speak English, and bunch of us have gathered around to make sure she don't remember.

"We think you been hanging around the reserve too long," we tell Constable Bobowski. "A man with long white hair, built like a super hero, that fit the description of a Windigo, a spirit man."

"We think you've had a significant vision," I tell her. "You've seen the Windigo more than once. We think we should take you to Etta's cabin. She'll make you some strong tea, make you feel better."

"You probably should take a year off, get acquainted with your spiritual self," Frank suggest.

Constable Bobowski groan. She look to Bedelia Coyote for support. Her and Bedelia are good friends, between them they responsible for opening a half-way house in Camrose for battered woman, and for starting up a Rape Crisis Line in Wetaskiwin. But there's business and there's family. This is family. Bedelia shrug her shoulders. "People who see the Windigo often have good medicine to offer. You should make that call on Etta."

"We'll be back," promise Constable Bobowski. A promise she'll certainly keep. And does. It ain't surprising that Ermine LaViolette has gone away with Einar Valgardson. What is surprising is who it was let the RCMP know Einar was on the reserve. We would of thought a jealous guy. Turn out it was a shy girl named Ruth Campfire, a not very pretty girl, who was in love with Einar, from a distance only, and decide that if she can't have him Ermine LaViolette won't either. Ruth Campfire read the newspapers every day and seen stories about how the police think Einar Valgardson, this fugitive from Iceland, might be hiding somewhere in Canada. She make the mistake of phoning the Immigration Department. They take three weeks to pass the information to the RCMP. What Einar wanted to do, instead of going into hiding, was go right to the RCMP, turn himself in and claim to be a political refugee, who being persecuted and can't get a fair trial in his own country.

From past experience, most people figure that would work. The Immigration Department keep mass murderers, rapists, terrorists, and other bad characters hanging around in the system forever, taking years and years to even give them hearings, while smarmy lawyers play the Immigration Department like an expensive musical instrument. "But what if it don't work? Einar's crimes aren't serious enough. He could get sent back," argue Ermine LaViolette, the one besides Einar, who have the most to lose.

It is one of these smarmy Immigration lawyers who point out the course of action we actually follow. He study the Indian Act for a few days and point out that there are provisions for Indians to adopt anyone of their choice into their tribe. That person become an actual Indian with all the rights and privileges of a natural born Indian. If that was to happen to Einar, he point out, he could stay at least on the reserve, and probably in the rest of Canada forever. The crimes he charged with in Iceland were the kind he couldn't be extradited for, if he was already a citizen of another country.

Everything move quite a bit slower than I've outlined. We hide Einar for several weeks, while the RCMP and the Immigration Department try (a) to find him, (b) by threats of all kinds of criminal charges, among them harboring a fugitive from justice, force us to tell where Einar was hid, (c) try to get charges laid against him that would predate any attempt to change his immigration status. Guess they must of read their own Indian Act. But all government departments move slower than water finding its own level.

Me and my friends get real excited the evening that Einar going to be adopted as an Ermineskin Indian. We seen these Indian blocades on TV, so me and Rufus Firstrider, Robert Coyote, a few other guys put bandannas over our faces, make it harder to breathe than you might imagine, take our .22 rifles and block off all the roads to the reserve. I don't know how Bedelia Coyote convince Chief Tom Crow-eye that this adoption is the thing to do. "Don't ask," are Bedelia's exact words, and she mumble about compromise, and you scratch my back and I'll scratch yours. My guess is that Bedelia is ready to run for a political office.

Einar Valgardson and Ermine LaViolette get a round of applause as they walk into Blue Quills Hall. Turn out they been hid right under our noses, right in Einar's bedroom at Mrs. Francine Fencepost's, the place no one attempt to look for them. Even Constable Bobowski never ask to look inside, she learned from experience that we always one step ahead of her and the other RCMPs, so she assumed Einar already hiding deep in the bush. Frank Fencepost is practically bursting with pride. "Silas, I keep my mouth shut all this time. I didn't think I could keep a secret, but I did. The hardest part was in the middle of the night listening to the bed springs creak in the next room, knowing Einar was doing to that beautiful girl, Ermine, what I been wanting to do ever since she reached ninth grade."

Chief Tom and Etta look at each other like they preparing to go ten rounds with one another in a boxing ring, but they keep their hostility at least skin deep, go ahead and perform whatever ceremony necessary to make Einar Valgardson a genuine Ermineskin Indian. Then everyone pass a peace pipe, and Einar give a thank you speech.

Then me and Bedelia head off to Wetaskiwin in Louis Coyote's pickup truck to tell Constable Greer of the RCMP what has happened, and see how the RCMP going to conduct themselves.

Mainly because of Constable Bobowski, they make three or four half-hearted attempts to have us turn Einar over to them. But all them and the Immigration Department do is make empty threats. Pretty soon Einar come out of hiding and nobody cause him any problems, and the next time treaty money come due there is a check for Yellow Bear Man, which the name Etta and Chief Tom give to Einar.

Just show how allegiances can change from minute to minute, while these other businesses are going on Eva McCarty is fighting for her and her kids to keep living on the reserve. Eva's story start more than a couple of years ago. Part of the Indian Act, a clause maybe 60 or 70 years old, state that a woman who marry a white man lose her status as an Indian forever. When she hear that Bedelia expand with anger like she been blown up by an air hose.

"That is so unfair!" she yell. I have to agree with her, as does almost everybody else, even Frank. Frank take pride in being a chauvinist pig when it comes to women's issues, and most of his opinions concerning women are a few hundred years behind the times, but even he realize that Eva McCarty being treated unfairly. Probably she should lose benefits while she's married to a white man, but after a divorce there's no reason she shouldn't be welcomed back to the reserve, and her children being half Indian should qualify, too. In fact the government departments involved agree that the children can stay on the reserve if they want to, but Eva can't because she gave up her all her rights as an Indian when she married. She can't leave her children behind.

Bedelia and a lady lawyer from Ponoka take weeks getting all the paperwork together to challenge the Indian Act, and it agreed that Eva can stay on until the case is decided. But then something happen and the story become what Bedelia call Page One News. At a national meeting of some kind, a gathering of Indian Chiefs from all across Canada, these chiefs are about 90% men, decide that granting Eva McCarty status would set a bad precedent. If they did, they say, there would a few thousand other Indian women wanting the same thing.

The case go through an Alberta Court, who rule that Indians can do whatever they please, and the court don't have any jurisdiction. The Alberta Supreme Court rule much the same, and the case now headed for the Supreme Court of Canada. Could drag on for a long time.

As time pass, someone suggest we do for Eva McCarty what we done for Einar Valgardson, but Chief Tom back off, saying Eva is already an Indian, can't adopt somebody who's already an Indian. What it amount to is Chief Tom and Samantha feel the same as the organization of Indian Chiefs, that if Eva get her way there could be a whole lot of other Indian women want the same thing.

After the dust is cleared away here's what we got. A woman who was born Indian and ain't changed a lick, is now, because of some crazy regulation, no longer considered an Indian and have to leave the reserve forever. A man with blond hair and blue eyes, who wasn't even born in North America, and who come to Canada because he is fugitive in his own country, is now officially considered an Indian, and immune from extradition for his crimes. A white man who lived as an Indian on the reserve for about ten years can't be kicked off, even though he's a troublemaker, because he ain't got no place else to go.

I throw up my hands and yell to Etta about how absurd all these events are.

"When elephants fight, the grass suffers," says Etta, shrug her buffalo-big shoulders.

First thing we need to take care of is Ermine LaViolette. "You'll put a spell on her, right?" says Frank. "Turn her into a mole, or a muskrat."

"Only desperate situations call for desperate actions like that," says Etta, look at Frank like he was a muskrat himself. There are lots easier ways.

Etta spend a lot of time watching CNN these days. Show how things have changed in even the last ten years. Then we didn't even have the electricity. Had to watch TV in the window of Robinson's Store in Wetaskiwin. Now people got electric stoves, refrigerators, VCRs, and life is just as weird as it ever was. Sometimes now, Etta, who may have a raccoon boiling in a kettle on the back of her stove, say to me, "Hurry up with your question, Oprah's coming on after this commercial." It was something that Etta learned from CNN that solved another of our problems.

Etta have me drive her down to Blue Quills Hall where she use a phone in the Band Office. I can't imagine who she would be talking to. "You can call in favors by phone, in person, or by thought process, whatever's easiest," Etta says when I ask her.

"Come see what I learned from TV," Etta says to me later on. Maybe she sent out word, or maybe she just thought hard, but Ermine LaViolette come knocking on her door that afternoon. "Silas here's my apprentice, and my witness," she say to Ermine. "Come on in, girl, sit down. I got a business proposition for you."

The proposition sure surprise me. Etta must of done some huge favors in the past. Ermine LaViolette is a really good barrel racer, so good she might be a champion on the big time rodeo circuit. What holding her back is a first class horse. Quality barrel racing horses are few and expensive.

There is a famous barrel racing champion named Sylvia Makes Her Own Medicine, who must now be pushing 40, has won the Cheyenne Rodeo and the Calgary Stampede championship more than once, and have the best barrel racing horse on the circuit, a black and white pinto that turn the figure-eights of barrel racing like he was greased and have feathers for hooves. I had no idea Etta even knew Sylvia Makes Her Own Medicine.

"I told her I had a vision," says Etta. "Said if she don't want to get hurt real bad she should retire. And when she retire I know just the person she should sell her pony to. I done her a big favor, a long time ago, when she was about Ermine LaViolette's age."

Ermine fidget on her chair, hardly touch the tea Etta serve her. She look suspicious at Etta, as a lot of young people do these days. After they've watched the *X-Files*, there ain't a lot Etta can do to surprise folks anymore. Her face lose some of its tension when Etta tell her that Sylvia will personally guarantee the loan she'll need to buy the pony, whose name is Black Shield. "And you don't have to pay nothing for the first six months while you getting established," Etta go on.

Ermine still looks a little suspicious. She knows that if a deal sounds too good to be true that it usually is.

"What do I gotta give back in return?" asks Ermine.

"Not much," says Etta.

"How much?" says Ermine.

"Not money," says Etta. "I figure with a successful career ahead of you, one where you gonna be on the road for ten months a year or more, mainly in the United States, a place where that big boyfriend of yours ain't legally allowed to go, that there ain't gonna be time in your life for a man."

Etta let that sink in for a while.

Ermine kind of grit her teeth, study the situation. She knows she can't leave her boyfriend behind, it only be human nature for him to get another woman.

She's just been offered something she been dreaming about for years, the thing she want most in life. Before she even speak it easy to see from her eyes, what lit with ambition, that giving up Einar Valgardson will be an easy thing to do.

"What do you want with him?" Ermine asks, genuinely puzzled.

"It'll all come out in the wash," says Etta.

"You know what I learn from watching CNN?" Etta ask another day.

"Besides there being a woman who have a hand that has a life of its own? She call the hand Joseph, and say 'Joseph, don't do that,' when the hand pinches her nipples."

"Besides that," says Etta.

"I heard on *Geraldo* that Mike Tyson and Michael Jackson are the same person, and only Lisa Marie can tell them apart."

"Besides that."

"I got no idea."

"I learned that everybody got a past that can be used against them. But, more interesting I learned that if you haven't got a past that can be used against you, you haven't lived enough to be of use to anybody. That's why men who've led clean enough lives to be eligible to run for office these day are about as exciting and as capable as mashed potatoes."

"I'm sure you're gonna make a point," I say, trying to be as sarcastic as Etta usually is with me.

"The point is, I been thinking about Gus Muskeg. Ask yourself why would a reasonably normal 40-year-old white man decide to come live on an Indian reserve permanently?"

"A woman," I answer real quick.

"Good answer. But wrong. Gus Munro came here alone. The first week he was here he was sleeping on the floor of Ben Stonebreaker's storage room. He start making cow eyes at Sadie Horseshoe, and she's lonely and take him in. Not that they don't make a good couple. I'm not saying that. What I am saying is that something else brought Gus Munro here, and my guess would be that he was running from something. Your friend, Constable Greer must owe you favor or two. Get him to check out Angus Munro."

"I always thought Gus stood for Gustave."

"You been wrong before," say Etta, smiling from way down deep in her face.

CNN sure does teach Etta a lot. I assure Constable Greer that the Angus Munro I want him to check out don't have anything to do with anyone either of us know.

"Of course not," says Constable Greer, tap his pipe full of Old Chum pipe tobacco.

He knows I am lying. And pretends to believe me. And, strangely, sometimes I do the same for him. A couple of weeks later he step out into the street and wave me into his office as I passing by RCMP headquarters in Wetaskiwin.

Constable Greer have about a five page FAX on his desk.

"This fellow Angus Munro, born Dec. 12, 1946, was a pretty bad actor. He's been in jail three times for writing bad checks, another time for theft, once for breaking and entering. But, I'd guess this fellow must be dead. He disappeared completely eleven years ago, just when he was due to face a whole lot of criminal charges. He ran a little used car lot, took vehicles on consignment, sold them for ridiculously low prices and pocketed all the cash, or drank it up, or gambled it away. He was looking at a long stretch when he disappeared. Probably walked into the river one dark night," and Constable Greer smile at me the way only one friend can smile at another.

I read the FAX to Etta.

"So, do we want him in jail, or do we want him silent?" Bedelia is also at this meeting.

"We just want him to stop being a shit disturber," says Bedelia.

"I'll have him over for tea," says Etta.

Next morning Etta says, "From now on he's gonna be known as Silent Gus." She smile big. "You can bet your joy stick on it."

"The first two problems taken care of. How you gonna fix up Eva McCarty's life?" I ask Etta. Eva not in any danger of being evicted for a while, but the stress of not knowing her future doing her some damage. I seen her down at the Alice Hotel bar more evenings than a single mom should be there.

"I'm most of the way there already," says Etta. "You don't think I got Ermine LaViolette that pony because I care two hoots about rodeo, do you?"

"I wondered about that."

"Good, shows there's some hope for you. You tell me what we're gonna do."

"You're gonna get Eva and Einar together."

"Good. Maybe one day I'll tell you some of the real secrets of being a medicine man. Only logical thing. Saturday night at Blue Quills there a box social to raise money to Molly Thunder's Dance Troupe. I gave Eva instructions on how to decorate her box lunch, and especially what to put inside it, even gave her hunk of my Christmas cake for dessert."

I groan. "I seen better stuff laying around corrals," I say, being sure to stay more than arms length when I say it.

"Medicine don't always taste good," says Etta. "I told Einar what that box gonna look like, but not whose it is. But he's gonna buy it, and after that nature more or less take its course."

Father Alphonse perform the wedding at Blue Quills Hall about three months later.

"If you think what comes over CNN is queer," Etta says to me while she's sitting in her tree-trunk chair at the back of the hall, me and her each enjoying a bottle of Lethbridge Pale Ale, waiting until the line get shorter before we congratulate the bride and groom. "We just seen a white man who is an Indian, marry an Indian who ain't an Indian, so she can become an Indian again."

"Do you think Oprah would be interested?"

"Too complicated," says Etta.

The Legend

This is a rodeo story. To begin it I have to go back almost twenty years to a time when I was barely born. I have to trust the memory of Mad Etta, our medicine lady, to fill in the details from long ago. I want to get the story down while the tragedy of it is still fresh in all our minds.

"Darcy Bloody Nose was as pretty a girl as ever come out of the reservation," Etta say. "But, oh, as they say, she had a mean streak a yard wide and mile deep. You seen her as a woman, well, she was as beautiful as a girl, but even more so. She always been tall and slim, have the prettiest head of hair I ever seen, heavy like a mane, black with a smear of scarlet through it, so in bright light her hair was like a sunset, black clouds dusted red by a setting sun.

"I remember the first time I realized she'd turned into a woman, she was leaning on the cattle chute down at the rodeo grounds, wearing tight jeans and a denim jacket, black boots that was soft as flannel. Her hair cover the back of her jacket, fall below her belt. She got fawn-colored skin and almond-shaped eyes. She leaning there in the sunshine smoking a cigarette, look about as sexy as any woman I ever seen, even on television.

"'Who's that?' I ask your ma, Suzie Ermineskin. Her and me was delivering a quilt we made down to Esaw Manyfeathers and his wife who got their camper parked behind the rodeo corral.

"'That's Hank and Lily's oldest. Darcy they call her. Pretty, eh?' your ma says.

"'I wasn't thinkin' that young,' I said. 'That looks like a growed up woman. Darcy Bloody Nose can't be more than fourteen.'

"'Just barely,' Suzy said. 'I hear she's mean as a snake. So pretty she can have any man she want. She been wipin' her feet on more than one guy this last few months.'

"Turn out she have her eyes on Phil Cardplayer the rodeo manager. Phil was twenty-seven or twenty-eight, married to a girl named Angella, come from way up North somewhere, was maybe an Athabasca Indian. They have twin boys, Alf and Zack, three or four years old, look like midget versions of their dad, built the same, walk the same, dress the same.

"Phil was one of them guys look like he was born in western clothes. He wear a white-on-white western shirt with pearl buttons, faded Levis with a big silver belt buckle he won at the Calgary Stampede when he was on the rodeo circuit. He wear a white hat with sweat stains, have a handsome, leathery face and a deep voice, send chills down the backs of all the pretty girls at the rodeos when he announce the events over the loudspeaker.

"I make a few inquiries," Etta go on, "and find that Darcy Bloody Nose don't care about anybody but herself. She is so beautiful and sexy, and available, no man she set out after going to stand a chance.

"'That girl gonna make one hell of a lot of enemies,' I say to your ma. 'She'll be lucky if some jealous woman don't slice her up like a ripe tomato.'

"But Darcy never seem to suffer any. It is Angella, that poor little Athabasca Indian who end up suffering. First of all Darcy move in on her man. There are lots of places around a rodeo for a couple to get together. Every tack room, hay loft, and borrowed camper get christened by their lust.

"Everybody know what's going on, except maybe Angella Cardplayer. And my guess is she knew exactly what was happening, only didn't have any idea how to handle it. Your friend Bedelia Coyote was a baby then too, if Angella had somebody like Bedelia to point out her rights things might have been a lot different.

"When they head off on the rodeo circuit that year, why Darcy all of a sudden have her own half ton with a camper. You can bet Phil must of used his own money to buy it for her. On the circuit Phil don't mind letting everybody see the situation. While Angella and the kids travel with him, he spend his nights in Darcy's camper. Folks say they make more noise having sex than some of the drunks who shout and play radios all night.

"I'm told there was a confrontation happen at the Rocky Mountain House Rodeo. Angella and Darcy meet up on the way to watch the bull riding.

"Angella is round faced and plump, dress like a traditional Indian woman, with a poncho and skirts and flat shoes.

"'You better stay away from my man,' Angella's supposed to have said. What else could she say, eh? Poor lady must of seen she was outclassed. Darcy was wearing an ivory-colored western shirt with red fringes, her scarlet-tinged hair fall down past the pockets of her jeans. Her cuffs are tucked inside those soft black boots have a big D hand tooled on each one.

"'Don't look like there's much of a contest here,' Darcy say, her eyes radiating pure hate. 'Phil already made his choice, now it's up to you to stop hanging around and cramping his style. Why don't you just pack up and go back to the reserve?'

"The conversation get fiercer as it go on. The surprising thing is Angella don't back down. She mention something about rodeo whores being a dime a dozen, make it plain she's willing to fight for her man. But Darcy ain't about to be drawed into a public fist fight. One she'd probably lose.

"'You're part of Phil's past,' Darcy says, staying well out of Angella's grasp. 'And there's not one fucking thing you can do about it.' Then she walk off, shaking her sexy bottom, and tossing that super long hair.

"There is a lot of speculation and argument about whether Phil have anything to do with what happen next. About half the people say, no way, the other half say, a guy who's got a hot girlfriend and is thinking mostly with his peter capable of doing anything.

"As I'm sure you know, Silas, there's lots of drugs around the rodeo circuit. Cowboys is generally hurt, and busy finding new ways of getting banged up every day. They always lookin' for painkillers, illegal or not, don't matter to them.

"This is the story I heard Angella Cardplayer tell in court, and Angella wasn't the type of person to lie. In their camper they kept a box full of medicines, everything from aspirin, analgesics, muscle bandages, to Indian herbs and potions, along with parts of left over prescriptions for painkillers, all the kind of stuff any cowboy with new bruises and sprains on top of old bruises and sprains would need. Everybody smoked marijuana in those days so it wouldn't be odd for there to be a joint or two in the box, just like there was always a bottle of whisky in the box to ease internal pain, or disinfect external wounds.

"About a week after her confrontation with Darcy, Angella was in a town called Rimbey. She'd put the boys to bed, and Phil had gone off to spend the night with Darcy, when a knock come to her door.

"'The guy at the door was a strange cowboy, but he was an Indian, so I trusted him,' Angella told the court.

"'He got his arm wrapped up tight in a surgical bandage.'

"'I think I dislocated my elbow,' he said, 'and Phil said you might have some painkiller.'

"'I got the box out from a cupboard,' Angella said, 'and this here strange cowboy rummage through it. He pick up part of a prescription Reynolds Cardinal got for his broken ribs, then he smile and take out a little bag of white powder from the box. There was two or three of those same plastic bags I never seen before. 'This here's good stuff,' the cowboy said. 'He'd already pocketed the pills used to belong to Reynolds Cardinal. He take a package of white powder, leave me two twenties and a ten, put them right into my hand.

"'You don't have to pay me,' I said. 'I don't even know what this stuff is, must be something new Phil got somewhere.

"'The cowboy must of given some kind of signal because three RCMPs burst through the door, fill up the whole camper. They got my hands handcuffed before I know what's what, and are telling me I'm drug trafficking. I don't even know what's going on. Turns out that strange Indian cowboy is an RCMP too.

"'What about my kids?' I keep saying. 'One of them RCMPs goes to the next camper, tells Julie Firstrider to look after my kids 'cause they taking me to jail.'

"You know, Silas, back in them days nobody really heard of cocaine, except as a rumor. These last few years I seen guys with big bags of it in the bars, hardly even hide it they're so bold.

"Because there was three packages there, they charge Angella with Cocaine for the Purpose of Trafficking. That was 'marked Money' the phony Indian RCMP give to her. She charged with the same for marijuana, and for selling painkillers, and reselling prescriptions.

"When the police contact Phil he say, 'I don't even live there, eh. Whatever she's doin' she doin' on her own.'

"Poor Angella, she's just an ignorant Indian girl from way up North. The newspaper make it sound like a major drug ring been broken at the rodeo grounds in Rimbey.

"The judge sentence her to ten years for traffic in cocaine, and a lot of small terms for the other offences, to run at the same time. The judge give a lecture about keeping evil drugs like cocaine out of Alberta, and say he making an example of Angella so others won't make the same mistake as her.

"Because it's such a long prison term, Angella get shipped off to Kingston Prison in Ontario, and since nobody have the money to go visit her she is pretty soon forgotten about.

"Before Darcy move in permanent with Phil, she make sure he knows she don't want them little boys, Leo and Zack, underfoot. And, Phil, thinking with his peter as always, send them off to his aunt who live on a reserve south of Calgary at a place called Gleichen.

"There just a couple more things you should know, Silas," Etta says to me. "After about five years, when she must of been almost eligible to get out, Angella escape from Kingston Prison. Apparently she knows where her twins are at, maybe she wrote to them, maybe not, or maybe she wrote and Phil's aunt never give them the letters.

"Leo and Zack Cardplayer been raised by that aunt who got a whole passel of kids herself. That whole family is involved in rodeo one way or another. Zack and Leo be ten or eleven by then and already taking after their dad by collecting trophies, belt buckles and ribbons for rodeoing. They both like bull riding the best, though they try their hand at all the rodeo events.

"The reason Angella escape is she is determined to see her boys. She hitchhike all the way west from Ontario, rob first a truck driver, then another man who give her a ride, hold a screwdriver against their throat while she take their money.

"In Medicine Hat, Angella rob another driver, steal his car, head hell-bent up the highway toward the reserve at Gleichen.

"The RCMPs are waiting for her near Gleichen, but she drive through a ditch past their roadblock, and they have to shoot out two of her car tires before they can stop her.

"She never actually get to see her sons, though one story have it that Zack and Leo hitchhike to Calgary, visit her in the jail there before she is shipped back to Ontario.

"Angella get sentenced to twice as many years in prison as before, this time for armed robberies, kidnapping, car theft, escaping custody, and all kinds of other charges."

I'm pretty well able to take the story from there. What Etta's told me I've heard in various forms of story, rumor, and gossip. Some of the versions I heard have Angella killing a couple of people during her escape, and that she robbed a bank in Ontario, and a government liquor store in Winnipeg.

Angella is pretty much a legend around these parts, though so is Darcy, but for different reasons. There is a ton of gossip whirl round Darcy's head, too. Like everyone figure she and maybe even Phil have something to do with Angella getting arrested in the first place.

After hearing the story I'm surprised that Phil and Darcy are still together. I would have figured Darcy for the type who would get tired of Phil in a few months and move on, probably to some bronc rider who'd treat her bad and swat her around every time he got drunk, or broke another bone at the rodeo.

"I'm the real legend around here," my friend Frank Fencepost say. "There are whores on 96th Street up in Edmonton, carve my name on wooden buildings." Since Frank's become pretty famous with his traveling gospel hour, we tease him that his name and FAX number are getting written on the walls of a better class of women's washroom these days.

"Hey, I had a good upbringing," Frank says. "When I was growing up I had a curfew that was very strictly enforced. I couldn't come home until after midnight."

A year or so after Angella been carted off to jail, Phil file a divorce, and when it come through he marry Darcy Bloody Nose, some say on the day she turn sixteen, though that may be gossip, too.

Some say that when Darcy look at Phil she see everything through a haze of dollar signs. That might be the truth, because over the years Phil get more and more successful. He invest in rodeo stock, land, range cattle, buy more land and lease it to wheat farmers. He now have a couple of sections over near Bittern Lake, supply a lot of livestock, bucking horses, and Brahma bulls, not only for the Alberta rodeo circuit but for the big rodeos in the United States, like Albuquerque, Cheyenne and San Antonio.

Phil still announce events at major Alberta rodeos, but him and Darcy travel in what must be a $90,000 air conditioned motor home, that fancier than any small town hotel or motel. In the winter they travel to some of the U.S. rodeos because Phil involved some way in promotion, and is maybe on the board of directors of the United States Professional Rodeo Association.

Phil and Darcy attend events called fund raisers, both for political parties, libraries and even the Wetaskiwin Art Gallery. Darcy get her picture in the *Wetaskiwin Times*. I seen her one night walking into the Travelodge banquet room, wearing a green, low cut dress, and she have the longest hair I think I ever seen. I heard it never been cut in her life and fall down most to her knees if left alone. It hard to believe but Darcy, they say, is only twenty-seven her last birthday.

They have a ranch house on a sidehill overlook Bittern Lake, built of varnished logs, have at least fifteen rooms, must be bigger, Frank Fencepost says, than Blue Quills Hall. There is a stone fireplace in the open-ceilinged living room, with shelves for Phil's rodeo trophies, and a buffalo head mounted so it look like the buffalo is standing in the next room with its head poked through the wall.

This is what I heard happened. To be fair there's more than one version. But, from what I've pieced together this appears the most likely. The boys, Leo and Zack, seventeen now, tall as Phil, look like mirror images of each other, appear on the doorstep, each holding his saddle on his right hip like a deformed child.

Phil welcomed them in, set them up in one of spare bedrooms.

I can't see no way to tell Leo and Zack apart. We sit with them one night at the Alice Hotel bar. Though they ain't of age they look twenty-five and the waiter never thinks to question them.

"We read each other's minds," the one who I think said he was Zack tells us. "We're both into bull riding, but we discovered we're good at the calf roping event. It takes two people, and we're two people, but we think like one.

"We fight like one really big person, too," says the one who may be Leo.

"That's good," says Frank. "This here reserve is so tough the Tooth Fairy carries mace."

"Our real mom's in jail," the Leo guy says all of a sudden, his face, that is wide and bland, crumpling up like a grocery sack been squeezed into a ball. "That woman at the ranch ain't our mother."

"Easy," Zack says to his brother. To us he says, "He's had a beer or two too many."

But, I know he ain't had but two glasses of beer, and it is seeing them side by side, Zack with his arm around Leo's shoulder that I understand they are really seventeen, a couple of overgrown kids who miss their mother.

Zack tells us then, how the minute they turn sixteen they borrow a cousin's camper truck and head off to rodeo in Ontario, and how they go to the prison to visit their mother.

But before that he tell us about what happened the time their mother escaped and tried to find them.

"After they took our mom away, we went out on the highway and hitched to Calgary. We was ten years old, and we'd been to Calgary maybe five times in our lives. The police told us they were taking her to something called the Calgary Remand Center, and once we got downtown we kept asking people where this place was until somebody showed us.

"We had to stand on tip toe to see over the desk. The policeman knew my mom's name, but he looked at us and said we was way too young to be let in to visit. And, he didn't even know if she was allowed visitors. 'You should speak to her lawyer,' he said. We didn't have any idea what he was talking about.

"But he turned out to be a nice guy. When he seen we was just hanging around the lobby of the remand center, he came around the counter and asked if we had a place to stay and if we had any money. I just kept shaking my head. Leo here was bawling.

"That policeman took his coffee break and walked us to the YMCA and paid for a room, give me some money for food and told me the time next morning when my mother would be out in the yard at the back of the building. Before he left us he made sure I knew how to use the key to my room, and that I knew my way back to the remand center.

"The next morning," Zack continue, "me and Leo went back to the remand center, and sure enough there was a half-dozen women walking around in the concrete yard, behind a high chainlink fence with rows of barbed wire all along its top.

"We're afraid to say anything. We stand shy and silent. Leo is crying, but quietly. One of the women spots us, but she don't show any emotion, just glances over to where two guards in sky-blue uniforms lean against a wall.

"We're down at alley level, the concrete yard and the bottom of the fence are about chest high for us. There are tall weeds cuddle up close to the fence. We have to peer through the dried weeds and stare across the floor at ankle level to the people inside.

"Though we been away from her for over half our lives, Leo recognize Mama. He grab the chainlink, shake the fence a little, call out her name. She hears him, glance our way, and when she sees us she runs the few steps over to the fence, grip onto what fingers Leo and I can poke through the chainlink.

"'I'd have knowed you guys anywhere,' she says, then she tells us how much she loves us and misses us.

"Mama's right eye is black, her cheeks are blue and swollen and there are ugly stitches across her forehead. 'Hit my head when the car crashed after they shot my tires,' she says, and makes a little smile even though we can see it hurts her to do that. 'Your mama's a regular outlaw, eh?'

"Then she go on to say, 'I don't care whether you understand it or not, I want to tell you what was done to me so that I end up in prison.' And she did.

"'I don't know if your father actually helped put me here, but there sure was lots of things he could have done to help me, which he didn't by staying silent and staying out of the way. I think he was just glad to get rid of me. My getting sent to jail was a lucky break for him.

"'I know it was Darcy Bloody Nose set me up. It was her got them to send that RCMP cowboy to buy medicine from me. It must of been her planted the drugs, too. I know she used to do drugs with some of the wildest cowboys, even after she was with your father.

"'To her, getting rid of me was just like scraping roadkill off the highway.'

"Mama sigh, and grip tighter on our fingers. 'I may never see you guys again, but I'm glad I tried. Whatever happens to me it was worth it.'

"Once, one of those guards started to walk over our way, but two or three of the other women step in front of her, and after a minute she go back to leaning against the wall, light herself a cigarette.

"Even when she get down on her knees, Mama couldn't get very close to us. We reach up to her, our faces at ground level, Mama almost lay down against the fence, while we push our faces hard against the metal wire. We're able to push our noses part way through, and Mama kiss the tips of our noses. All these years later, now I'm grown up, I still wake up in the night feeling the warmth of Mama's lips on my nose."

"We're gonna do something," Leo says.

"No, we're not," says Zack. "Can't hold his liquor," he says of Leo, giving us most of a smile.

They did do something, of course. Just a few weeks later.

I can see them deciding, thinking with the same brain — we'll do this to our father, this to Darcy, his new wife. It must have taken them a long time to make their decisions. My guess is Zack would make the suggestions, and Leo would think about them for a while, maybe a long while, before nodding, or adding to, or changing the plan a little to the right or left.

The story Zack and Leo told everyone went like this. The twins was sitting one on each side of their father on the corral fence, admiring their meanest Brahma bull, name of Vengeance, who trot around the corral, snort, paw the ground, look for something to hurt with his crooked horns.

While the three of them was sitting there, their step-mother, Darcy, come walking down from the house. She was wearing a long, scarlet robe, her hair loose and streaming down her back.

It is about this time that their father, who been complaining since supper that he wasn't feeling good, pass out in a faint, fall into the corral, right in front of Vengeance the bull.

Vengeance stick a horn in their father's back before the boys can do anything. They both leap into the corral, try to attract the bull's attention, draw him away from their father, but the bull gore Phil again, then turn on Zack toss him in the air over his shoulder, do him quite a bit of damage.

The boys say this all take about ten seconds to happen.

At this point, as the bull is turning from Zack back to Phil, Darcy climb between the rails, calm as you please, swish the skirts of her scarlet robe at the bull, succeed where the twins fail to draw the bull's attention away from Phil Cardplayer.

If she'd only taken off the robe, they said, used it like a bullfighter's cape, everything might have turned out okay. Darcy, they said, was only worried about Phil, not herself. While she is drawing the bull out to the middle of the corral, Leo drag his unconscious father under the bottom rail, then go back to rescue Zack, who is crawling toward the fence, and whose leg they figure is broke, though it turn out to be just a super bad charley horse.

With his father and Zack safe, Leo turn to the middle of the corral where he see a terrible thing happening. The bull has picked Darcy up on his crooked horns, toss her in the air like she was a scarecrow, catch her as she coming down, toss her again.

After she caught on his horns, he charge across the corral, ram her and his head straight into the corral fence. Leo say that is the only time Darcy make a sound, a scream like a rabbit make when it first been wounded.

Leo make his way back into the corral, this time with a saddle blanket, but what's happened now is even worse. Darcy's long hair has tangled around the bull's crooked horns, so now he is charging around trying to shake her off his head and not having any luck.

When Leo see he can't be any help in the corral he run to the pickup for a rifle. Darcy was still alive, Leo say, because she say something to him, maybe it was Help Me! maybe it wasn't. He rest the rifle on the top rail, take careful aim, shoot the bull in the heart. It crash to the ground, pinning Darcy right to the earth. By the time Leo gets to her she is dead.

Phil has come conscious by now and is bleeding pretty bad. All Leo can do is call 911 for an ambulance, tell Phil how Darcy saved his life, and probably Zack's too.

Phil he die at the hospital a few hours later before the RCMP get a chance to talk to him.

That is the official version that Leo and Zack tell around, and that Constable Greer of the RCMP let me look at in his office one day, even though he's not supposed to. But, Constable Greer say, there is more questions unanswered than answered.

What else might have happened?

Me and Frank and Etta speculate up a couple of ideas. We are the only ones hear Leo say him and Zack was planning something. Nobody, including the RCMP ever ask us any questions, not that we'd have remembered what Leo said anyway.

First of all, none of us think Darcy walked into the corral on her own. What she always liked about rodeo was the cowboys, *after* they was finished for the day and ready to party. If she would of come to the corral, which wasn't likely, she would have been wearing Levis and boots, not a silky robe and slippers.

One way we think it might have happened is for Zack or Leo to knock Phil across the back of the neck with a piece of firewood, let him fall forward on his face, leave him for the Brahma bull to have a few pokes at with his crooked horns.

We suspect the boys either carry Darcy down from the house, or force her to walk there while they hold a gun on her. We also suspect they give her a choice of walking into the corral or getting shot.

Another way it may of happened is mainly Etta's idea. A couple of days after, when the RCMP get through with the place, Etta have me drive her out there to the ranch. The place is quiet as nighttime, don't seem to be no birds singing, though I guess maybe the ranch is always this quiet.

Etta waddle around the corral, spend a long time up toward the cattle shed studying the gate people use to enter and leave the corral, the long, swinging gate where cattle herded in and out. Then she study the cattle chute and stall where the bull or bucking bronc stored just before it released into the corral.

"Tell me something, Silas," says Etta. "If you was at the house and taking a leisurely walk down to the corral, never suspecting anything was wrong, would you go to the people gate or the cattle gate?"

I look the situation over because I know this is probably a trick question.

"It would be shorter to come to the people gate, and more logical. Plus, Phil and the boys were sitting on the fence near the people gate."

"Do we know that's true?"

"The top pole of the fence is polished some from people sitting on it regularly. Below are cigarette butts, burned matches and an empty tin of Skoal. Anybody can see that section of fence was a favorite watching place."

"Good. You're about half as smart as you could be."

I'm not sure if that is a compliment or not.

"What I seen down there," and she point to the cattle gate, "is some of Darcy's long hair caught in the rough lumber."

"That could have happened if she ran into the corral the way Leo said."

"Hmmmph!" says Etta.

She beckon me with one of her sausage fingers to follow her over to the chute where they release the bull, calf, or bucking bronc that is to be wrestled or roped.

"Look here," says Etta. "Darcy's long hairs are on this gate, too. How do you explain that?"

I shrug my shoulders.

"Means Darcy was inside this here chute. She was supposed to be in the middle or at the other end of the corral, drawing the bull away from Phil and Zack."

"Maybe when the bull was tossing her around he banged her against the gate."

"On the inside?"

"Could the gate have been open?"

"A possibility. The kind of thing a smart lawyer would bring up in court. The possibility exists, no matter how unlikely."

"What's your explanation?"

"First let's follow the scrape marks, see where they drug the body of the Brahma bull to."

I'm not very keen on that but I walk along behind Etta the length of the cattle shed, down a grassy knoll and into a garbage dump, below and downwind from the house. The bull lying on the edge of a manure pile, stiff legged, his neck twisted over his shoulder. As we get closer we can hear the sound of flies buzzing. Big blow flies are all around the carcass, their bodies blue and shiny like flying boxcar airplanes. A few magpies and a crow been sampling the body. The crow fly to a nearby tree and caw at us. The magpies, black and white as old photographs, back away just out of reach, dare us to do anything to them.

Etta waddle right up to the carcass, stare at it for a while. Move around, look at it from as many angles as possible without getting manure on her shoes.

"Look here," she says.

"I'd rather not," I say. "I don't like the smell of death."

"The bull's dead. It can't do you no harm," Etta say, real cross. "Everything dies."

I move up and stand behind her. One of the bull's cloudy eyes is staring crazily at the sky. My stomach do a little flip.

"See here," says Etta, "there's hairs wrapped around the horns."

"Bull tossed her around like a rag doll. Wouldn't that be natural?"

"I didn't say 'caught on her horns.' I said 'wrapped around.'"

I know Etta is going to explain her idea. I back slowly away from the carcass with short steps.

"I think there's a lot more went on than anyone suspects," says Etta. "You don't even know your own history, Silas. I don't mean from the time the white men come to the prairies, I mean long, long before, that time when truth, history and dream all blend together.

"What I think happened at the corral took a lot longer than anybody let on. I think that back in Ontario, at the Kingston Prison, Zack and Leo and their mother hold a kind of trial, find Darcy guilty, find Phil probably guilty but enough to give him a chance. They whack his head, let him fall into the corral, let fate and nature decide whether the bull go after him or not.

"With Darcy they help nature along. I bet that after the bull lost interest in Phil after doing him quite a bit of damage, the boys rope it and lead it into the chute. Can't be sure whether they overpowered Darcy, which would have been easy 'cause they're big men, or just held a gun on her. I think when they got the bull in the chute, they blindfolded him to keep him calm, then they make Darcy hang on to the gate of the chute while they tie her long hair to the bull's horns. Then they unblindfold the bull, throw open the gate and let him do what they will with Darcy."

"That seem far fetched to me."

"It would because you don't know your history. There's a story, hundreds of years old, about an evil woman who was tied by her hair to the horns of a bull. The bull toss her around until she's dead."

I still don't think much of the idea.

"How would Zack and Leo know about stuff like that. They only went to school when they couldn't get out of it. I bet neither of them ever read a book don't have a centerfold in it."

"You forget about their mother. She's had years to read up on myths and legends."

"You think she put the boys up to it?"

"Give me a better explanation and I'll believe *you*."

"Why wouldn't the RCMP suspect?"

"You forget, Darcy died a hero. Heroes don't get murdered. And these young people from the RCMP are city people, don't speak Cree and mangle what English they know. Also, you don't find something you not looking for."

That's the way things stand.

The house is closed up now. A caretaker live in the bunkhouse and the land is leased out to one of the Overholtzer brothers. Zack and Leo only show up once a year for a day or two when the rodeo season is on. They both live in Ontario, visit their mother regular, say they is saving the place for her when she get out of prison, which may be in as little as a year or two.

Fun and Games

I f there are some things me and Frank ain't, it's athletes. I got the build for sports, I'm tall and thin and look like I could run real fast and generally be good at basketball, baseball and football. Unfortunately, when I run my feet sort of kick out to the side, and when it come to games played with a ball I got what are called concrete hands, couldn't catch anything to save my life. Frank Fencepost on the other hand, think he can do anything. Even though he can't skate, Frank figure he could out-play Wayne Gretzky at hockey if only he put his mind to it, and figures he could play baseball, football, tennis, or figure skate with the best of them if he just practised for a few days.

The way we get to this city called Victoria, is that I get invited to read for an audience in a literary festival during the Commonwealth Games, which near as I can figure is Canada's version of a poor man's Olympics. These games involve countries never win much of nothing in the Olympics because the United States and the ununited states that used to be Russia beat up on everybody else.

Also, the Queen of England is supposed to be queen of the Commonwealth, but I see by the newspaper there are countries participating like Brunei, which far as I know, is a rich Arab island where the sultan is worth about a zillion dollars, and places like Sri Lanka, Malasia, Botswana, Sierra Leonne, and parts of countries like Jersey and Guernsey, which are cows and islands but not countries. Then there is Cyprus, which is a place Greece and Turkey been fighting over for a hundred years, and a dozen or so countries I never heard of, like Nauru, and Norfolk Island. Looks like to be in the Commonwealth Games all you got to do is be an orphaned country and have some athletes, or what pass for athletes.

"I figure I'll enter myself in a couple of those sports while we're there," says Frank, "win a couple of medals for Hobbema, just to pass the time. Maybe boxing. I've watched Olympic boxing on TV, a back-to-school sale at the Hudson's Bay Department Store in Edmonton is more dangerous."

"I have to agree," I say. "Olympic boxing is about the sissiest sport there is. There's more body contact in synchronized swimming."

What I don't say is, what would be good about Olympic boxing for Frank is that the loser always seems to win. The rules have nothing to do with fighting, if you was to cover up and let the other guy hit you for three rounds, you'd be sure to win the decision. Frank would be good at that.

Me and Frank are walking around downtown Victoria, which is on an island off the west coast of Canada, across the Rocky Mountains from where we live. We are in a place called Bastion Square, which have lots of little shops, the square itself decorated for the games with banners blowing in the wind, making noise like snapping fingers.

There are lots of athletes walking around in their colorful jackets. A whole group of people about our age, three men and three women, come up to us as we leaning against a wall in the sunshine.

"You are from what country, please?" a girl with a big wide smile say to us. She is tall and healthy looking, with sand-colored skin and black eyes.

"We are from Canada," says Frank in his best evangelist voice, pound his chest a couple of times for emphasis. "We are, my friend Nathan Esquimalt here, and me, original genuine aboriginal people of Canada. Want to see me carve a totem pole?"

"We might have a unique . . . " the girl begin.

"I could blockade a highway right before your very eyes. It is in our blood, like hunting buffalo, and playing bingo."

The little group ignore Frank. The smiling girl, who appear to be spokesman for the group continue.

" . . . and very versatile and profitable proposition to make with you." The young woman introduce himself as Sabatt, or something close. Some of the others are Ari and Ali and longer names I don't remember for even a second. Her accent is pretty strong, her voice high pitched and sing-songy.

Frank look that girl up and down.

"Is it illegal?"

"Would we be dealing with persons such as yourselves, who appear to be of an inferior class of vagrant, if our business was not of the type considered illegal in many jurisdictions?" says the fellow named Ari, whose ribs show through his thin shirt, and don't look like he's had a good meal since Trudeau was Prime Minister.

"Good point," says Frank. "So what's the scam?"

There are three days before I am to do my public reading. The games open tonight, and from TV I learn that there is supposed to be a big parade ending with the lighting of the game flame. On television, the athletes from other countries getting ready to march in a few hours. Each group dressed in jackets with their national colors and carrying a banner with their country's name on it.

"We should be in the parade," says Frank.

I point out that Canada as host country have the biggest contingent of athletes. "All these people waving Canadian flags and wearing red and white jackets with maple leaves and, is that a Canada goose on them? are Canadians."

"No. No. I mean *we* should be in the parade. You and me. We'll represent the country of Hobbema."

"Might be a little hard to pull off."

"Silas, how many times do I have to tell you, in order to get what you want all you got to do is look the part? Across the street there is a sign company. See, they do lettering, billboards, neons, signs on walls. What kind of reaction do you think we'd get if we rushed in there and asked for an instant sign for the parade for the country of Hobbema?"

"They'd toss us out on the street."

"That's right, they would. If they thought we were a couple of Canadian Indians pulling a scam. But, we're not."

"We're not?"

"No. We're from Hobbema, a small country a world away from Canada." Frank talks like a friend of ours in Wetaskiwin named Pindar, who is from Bangladesh, and who manage the Wheatlands Motel. Frank takes off his black, ten-gallon hat, snatches off mine, arranges to leave them behind the counter of a restaurant. We go to the restaurant washroom where Frank undo his braids, slick back his long hair with water, while I do the same.

"Just follow my lead," says Frank. "Let Brother Frank lead you down the path of righteousness."

"Your path of righteousness usually leads directly to jail."

"Ah, but before we get there we will pass GO and collect more than two hundred dollars. Trust your personal evangelist," says Frank.

"Good morning, please," Frank says to the receptionist at the sign shop. "We have for you a rush order must be completed in time for the Commonwealth Games parade, yes?"

The receptionist call somebody out from the back of the shop.

Frank bows to the fellow who is gray-haired, wear coveralls, hold a small paintbrush in his hand.

"We have arrived moments ago in your beautiful country, and require a sign for the parade which is about to happen."

"We're pretty busy, eh," the guy says.

"We require only our country name on a signboard, please. The country is H-O-B-B-E-M-A."

"Where's that?"

"We are across the world from you, yes? But, we bring with us much goodwill and many greetings from the Sultan of Hobbema, who has authorized us to pay you many *braegels*, which is our unit of currency, in return for a sign."

The guy shows a little interest.

"How much are these *bagels* worth?"

"I believe the Sultan said a braegel is worth about half a dollar. We will think nothing of paying you one thousand *braegels* for the sign we require."

The sign man calculate in his head for a while, then smile, but not enough to let us know he is about to cheat us.

"Your sign will be ready in thirty minutes, eh."

"You will notice that my friend and I, my friend is a eunuch in charge of the Sultan's harem — you know what that is, please? He still has the gearshift, but lacks the gears. Yes, very humorous. He is able to run very fast, yes. Very fast. We are dressed in the garb of true Westerners are we not? In our country our national heroes are Roy Rogers and his faithful horse, Dale Evans. Do you perhaps have acquaintance with them personally, so you could introduce us?"

"Roy Rogers?" says the sign man. "Roy Rogers is an old cowboy, must be pushing ninety. His horse is Trigger — I hear he had Trigger stuffed and displayed in a glass case. His wife is Dale Evans. She's as old as he is. They own some sandwich shops or something."

"Oh, excuse my ignorance," says Frank. "Language barriers sometimes cause me much embarrassment. Perhaps you could introduce us also to Garth Brooks and Reba McEntire? In Hobbema, Roy Rogers remains forever youthful by means of film, as do his horse and his wife whichever they may be, as well as his many-whiskered but amiable companion. We could pay you handsomely in braegels for such an introduction."

"I'll see what I can do, eh?" the sign man says. We can feel his greed filling the air like swarms of gnats.

When he returns with the sign, Frank offers him a choice.

"Please to pick from these samples of your colorful currency an amount sufficient for your needs."

What Frank offer is about seventy-five dollars in twos, fives and tens.

"I thought you said a thousand bagels, or whatever."

"Ah, yes, you are very shrewd. If you will make out an invoice, please, my assistant will deliver it to the Sultan's suite at the Empress Hotel. The Sultan of Hobbema has two floors reserved for he and his many wives. Would you prefer to exchange the money at your own bank, or should we convert it to Canadian dollars in advance?"

"I'd like good old Canadian money, eh."

"Consider it done," says Frank.

We head off to the parade carrying our sign.

"Greed is the great equalizer, Silas. Offer people something too good to be true and they'll grab for it. I'd have paid him seventy-five dollars for a fifty dollar sign, but he wants to take a poor tourist for five hundred dollars."

The athletes march alphabetically. We wait at the side of the road, leap in somewhere between Ghana and Honduras, march right along wave to the crowd.

The scam that Ari and his friends want to pull is that they want to stay permanently in Canada. Zarina, the girl who first spoke to us and Ari want to exchange places with us. They want to buy all our identification, birth certificates, drivers licenses, social insurance, medical insurance, video rentals, library cards, even credit cards — like we'd have credit cards. In return they will give us a pile of money and their identification from some country we never heard of, that is only slightly larger than a postage stamp, and whose main export is oil, and revolution. Zarina says there is an oil well every hundred yards and the national sports are slapping sand flies, dodging scorpions, and trying to keep track of who is in power, the government or the insurgents.

Frank and me hold a quick confab.

"We can report our ID lost or stolen and get it all replaced," says Frank. "Let's see if these guys really got money."

Frank name a figure about five times what Ari has suggested and add *each* after it.

Now it is their turn to put their heads together. We take them into a cocktail lounge, introduce them to tequila sunrises.

They have never had alcohol before. It is against the law in their country. "If we are going to live here we must learn the customs of the country," says Ali, who is short and muscular, claim to be on his country's wrestling team. After two tequila sunrises each they are much easier to negotiate with.

When we part, our wallets are stuffed with hundred dollar bills and their pockets are full of Canadian ID. Frank and Ari exchange ID. Me and Zarina do the same. I tell her she will have to develop a deep voice if she's going to be Silas Ermineskin from now on, but I don't think she quite understands.

Zarina and Ari, who if I understand them right, are cousins, decide to wait around until the rest of their friends are able to buy ID. They can't go back to their hotel so we put them up in my room at the Delta Hotel on the waterfront, where I been given a room for three days because of the reading I'm going to do.

The next morning the headline in the *Victoria Times-Colonist* read:

ELEVEN ATHLETES MISSING FROM COMMONWEALTH GAMES

I would guess that all eleven are in our room, plus a few people we met at the bars last night.

"I was once kicked in the face by a goat," says Ali, "afterward I did not feel nearly this bad."

"Welcome to Hangover City," says Frank. "I feel sorry for people who don't drink," Frank go on, "when they wake up in the morning, they feel as good as they're going to feel all day."

"No wonder they do not allow alcohol in our country," says Zarina, holding her head. She went into the walk-in closet with a good looking fellow who is maybe named Farook, and they didn't come out for about seven hours.

Some of the other people scored ID in the bars last night. They argue about whether to leave Victoria now, or wait for the big exodus at the end of the games.

An interesting thing happen to us after we walk in the parade. There are thousands of people milling about when the parade break up, while we still staring around and carrying our sign a couple of girls come up to us. They are white Canadian through and through, one is white blond and one is golden blond and they make it plain they'd like to know us better. If they knew we were real Indians from Alberta they'd look through us like we didn't exist.

"Ah, yes, pretty ladies," says Frank, "I am the personal assistant of the Sultan of Hobbema, the Sultan is a man of great generosity. Frank reach in his pocket and pull out the roll of hundred dollar bills. Whatever I spend the Sultan will replace in the morning. He has been known to chastize me for not spending enough money. This is like the bottomless glass which is not half empty but half full, yes."

Our new friends agree. But I can read Frank's mind. He is thinking of somehow losing me and claiming both women for himself. Frank can't help himself. There is something about pretty girls; his hormones take over and his brains turn to mush.

"It is a shame that my companion here, who is known as the tall and silent one in our language, is the attendant of the Sultan's harem, and you know . . . "

I take a hold of Frank's left wrist and squeeze to attract his attention. I squeeze until I imagine I can feel twigs snapping inside, and Frank's face take on a bluish tinge. Frank get the message, his brain untangle some, and he continue right on with what he was saying, only I know he has made a giant switch in his story.

"... as he is exposed to the most beautiful women in the world every day, therefore it is quite an honor for you peasant girls to attract his attention. Need I mention that he has even more spending money than I, and that he is most anxious to see the interiors of your most respected restaurants and night clubs."

Frank hold his left wrist with his right hand, bend it gingerly back and forth to be sure nothing is broken.

"The Devil made Brother Frank do it," he whisper to me. The girls are named Bonnie and Dierdre and come from a town called Sooke, a suburb of Victoria. It took me a minute to figure they weren't saying something sexual when they first mention the town.

We eat at a revolving restaurant overlooking the harbor. Frank still carrying the sign say HOBBEMA. He use it as a bribe of some kind. Him and me sign it and give it to the guy in the shiny wine-colored tuxedo who wear a badge say Maitre de Hotel. In return for the sign the wine flow to our table all night and the bill don't.

Bonnie and Dierdre like to tell blond jokes.

"What do you do when a blond needs a refill?" Dierdre ask, waving her empty glass. "You blow in her ear."

"How does a blond turn on the light after she'd had sex? She opens the car door."

"How can you tell if a blond's been using your computer? There's white-out on the screen."

"How does a blond pull up her sox? She pulls down her jeans so she can get at them."

"Why do blonds wear panties? To keep their ankles warm."

"Why do blonds have square breasts? They forget to take the tissue out of the box."

"How do you get a blond to marry you? Tell her she's pregnant."

"What's the first thing a blond asks the doctor after he tells her she's pregnant? Is it mine?"

We take in a couple more clubs, end up back at the girls' apartment where there is never much doubt about what going to happen.

"There is a reason we are called athletes," Frank puffs, as his girl finishes screaming with pleasure, and says she wishes Canadian boys knew some of the tricks he does. Dierdre thinks treating the favorite part of my anatomy as if it was a birch tree and she was a beaver, is the way to go. I am close to yelling, though it ain't from pleasure.

"When we get across the water we are going to take a taxi to Montreal, to where I have many friends and relatives, all refugees from economic hardship, who will hide me," says Ari.

"All in Canada illegally?" says Frank.

"Of course. To us of the third world Canada is like an unguarded orchard with a wide variety of fruits there for the taking."

"I hate to disillusion you, but have you looked at a map lately?" I ask. "You're gonna need a ton of taxi money to get to Montreal."

"How far you figure it is?" Frank ask the guy we call Ali.

"Surely not more than one hundred kilometers."

"We don't deal in kilometers," I say, "but I'd guess it's about three thousand miles, which is a whole lot more in kilometers."

"Well, gracious goodness," says Farook, "we shall have to alter our plans. Is it possible that we could sail there?"

We count their money for them, guess at plane fares, and decide they ridin' the old gray dog to Montreal.

"Goodbye, Ari, goodbye, Zarina," say Ari and Zarina at the bus depot.

"Goodbye, Silas, goodbye, Frank," we say.

"Well, we've given up our identity," I say, as the ferry to Vancouver pull out. "We've now got names we can't pronounce, and come from a country we never heard of. And, we're each entered in two events at the Commonwealth Games."

"The next few days are gonna be all fun and games," says Frank, dancing sideways across the parking lot at the ferry terminal.

Do I need to tell you that the next batch of trouble we get into was Frank's idea? Ari and Ali and their friends make it sound like the easiest thing in the world is to obtain political asylum in Canada.

"They allow you to go on welfare forever, bring the rest of your family to Canada and put them on welfare, too," said Ari. "My friends in Montreal write glowing reports on the generosity of the Canadian system. In our country the average wage, if one was to work, would be $85 dollars a year. In Montreal my friend receives fifteen times that every month for sitting in the park watching the fleur-de-lis grow."

"We would like to apply for political asylum in Canada, please," says Frank.

"Or Quebec, please," I say, adding, *La nez de ma tante dans la poche de mon oncle,* which is about the only French I know.

The immigration guy sure stare at me strange. He is a sad looking little man, weight about 120 pounds, got a baggy blue uniform make him look like a bus driver been unemployed for ten years. He have baby blue eyes and a few strands of thin red hair fall across his forehead.

"You're one of these athletes, right?" He don't wait for an answer. "You'd be #7 and #8 out of eleven. Do you have a criminal record in your country? Any outstanding warrants?" he say in a tired voice, as if he doesn't care in the slightest.

We both say, no.

"That's too bad," say the sorry little man. "If you were a fugitive in your own country, you'd be certain to be admitted as an immigrant here. Canada would never send a criminal back to a country where he might be imprisoned for his crime."

"Oh," Franks says, "I misunderstood the question. I thought you said phonograph record. And I got great warrants, I guess you could say outstanding if you wanted to. I know at least two dozen girls will back me up. Much to my chagrin I left my phonograph records behind in my own country. But if it is a criminal you want, yes, please, the police in my country are irritated with me because I blew up with explosives our country's only oil refinery in order to protect the environment, the little fishes, birds, animals and trees, yes?"

"Now we're getting somewhere," says the Immigration guy. "Please describe the nature of your crimes, and whether they have political implications. Do you fear to return to your own country because you may be unfairly persecuted because of your political or religious beliefs?"

We answer yes to those questions and try to say whatever that little man might like to hear. He fill out a long blue form for each of us, send us down the hall where we sit in a waiting room full of people look like they stepped out of a Coke commercial.

"I bet if we was all to sing 'We are the World', it would improve our chances," says Frank. He start in to hum. He has all the singing ability of a billy goat.

"They've convened a special panel," say one of the athletes, who speak pretty good English. "They will deal with us before the games are over, so that if rejected we may return with our peers to our proper country."

Six of us claimants sit around the bottom end a big oval oak table. The immigration panel sit at the other end, five people: two white men and a white lady, an East Indian man, and an Asian woman, hard to guess what persuasion. There are also two lawyers, one, a big-bellied man in a blue suit, is for the government, and the another, a skinny lady with her hair in braids, look like most of her clothes are crocheted, have a baby in a basket that she connect to one of her breasts every time it whimper. The breast-feeding lady seem to represent all six of us, whether we want her or not.

Frank's passport have about six unpronounceable names on it, the only way he can be sure they're talking to him is when they point at him.

"Your passport photo bears you little resemblance, Mr. El-Halizar," the East Indian man says to Frank.

"Just call me Frank. That's my New-Canadian name. I'm told it means honest and forthright, which is appropriate, for that's what I am."

"In that case, perhaps you could answer my question?"

"You know what passport photos are like. You must have had one taken. In my former country there is only one camera, guy who use it have to hide his head under a black rag and set off a firecracker to get it to work. I'm just lucky there a picture there at all."

I'm waiting for them to comment on my photo, which not only don't look anything like me, but is of a woman. But I guess that is only obvious to me. They ask me a few simple questions, and I admit I'm not a criminal, have never been in jail, and though I try to say I'm afraid to go back because I believe in Democracy, and the Military Dictatorship in my country don't approve of people like me, I'm afraid my heart isn't in it.

"Mr. El-Halizar," the Asian lady say to Frank, "in what ways do you think you could contribute to making Canada a better place?"

A loaded question, if I ever heard one. This is Frank's chance to brag about his sexual prowess. But, as always, Frank surprise me.

"It has taken great dedication for me to reach the pinnacle of success as a swimmer," Frank replies. "I feel that I can transfer that success to Canada. I may well be able to represent, and bring glory to Canada, for many years to come in national swimming championships, the Commonwealth Games, and perhaps, even the Olympics."

Everyone at the power end of the table look pleased, except the Asian lady.

"Mr. El-Halizar, my records indicate that you are a pole vaulter, not a swimmer."

"I'm the swimmer," I whisper to Frank. I hope I don't have to put on a demonstration. I'm so afraid of water I only fill my teacup half full.

"It is a custom in my country never to brag on one's own accomplishments. That is considered very bad form. What I have done is spoken for my less fortunate friend here beside me," and Frank pat my shoulder. "My friend is not nearly so accomplished an athlete as I, therefore I am worried that you will not treat him with every consideration, unlike myself, in whom I have every confidence of your goodwill."

I have to admit Frank has a natural gift for bafflegab.

The interviews go on for hours, then we have to go back to the waiting room. We are tired and sweaty and I'm just anxious to get back to the hotel and shower. But, when I try to leave I find the door is locked.

"Why can't I go?" I ask the guy in a brown uniform who sit by the door.

"Because you're an illegal alien. You can't go anywhere. If you're not approved as a refugee, you'll be deported."

"But I'm a . . ." Canadian I start to say. But my ID is with Zarina on its way to Montreal, and I don't know a single person in Victoria who would recognize me. Maybe the man who own Munro's Book Store on Government Street, I signed my books there yesterday . . .

Finally, the lady lawyer with the baby at her breast come out to say we all been approved but me. "You are considered an economic refugee not a political refugee. You have the option of returning to your own country and applying for Landed Immigrant status through regular diplomatic channels."

So, I been turned down as an immigrant to my own country because I'm not dangerous enough. Frank get to stay because he's a criminal. Everybody else get to leave, I'm gonna be held in detention.

"Fingerprints," I say to Frank. "RCMP in Alberta got my fingerprints. You got me into this, you got to get me out."

"Hey! Has Ari El-Halizar ever let you down?" Frank ask.

Mother's Day

S uicide is the meanest kind of grief," says Etta our medicine lady, "somebody dies of disease or gets killed in a car accident we know how to act. We cry, we tell the survivors how sorry we are, we send flowers, we take food to the house. We attend the funeral. Suicide is so different, most of us, even me, don't know how to act. So don't feel bad. You're not alone with being uncomfortable with suicide."

I'd asked Etta a question about whether I should even go to Benny White Hand's funeral. I didn't really want to, though I'd known Benny all his life, and his mother, Madelaine White Hand is one of the kindest and nicest women I know.

Benny White Hand killed himself last weekend. On one of the meanest days in February when there are puddles of ice after a chinook and a saw-toothed wind figure to cut you in half, he walked into the woods carrying a pail and a rope. He turned the pail over, stood on it, tied the rope to a big branch of a spruce tree, put the other end around his neck and kicked the pail over. Benny White Hand was nineteen years old.

While he wasn't one of our close friends, me and everybody in our group knew him. He'd sometimes hang around Hobbema Pool Hall and Ben Stonebreaker's General store.

His mom is a school teacher and she always liked it when a bunch of us would come to her house of an evening or a Saturday afternoon. She'd make popcorn and when we were younger always had Kool-Ade, and later on Coke, 7-Up, and Orange Crush for us to drink.

Mrs. W., as we call her, is a tall rawboned woman with deep set eyes and black hair that goes every which way no matter how much hair spray she soak it down with. She has the jolliest laugh in three provinces. I bet sometimes you could hear her all the way down the hill to Hobbema Pool Hall which must be six or seven city blocks. Frank Fencepost would say something like, "Chief Tom is living proof that the gene pool needs more chlorine," and while me and my friends would laugh, Mrs. W. would positively whoop. She would slap her thigh like somebody in a bar, not like a school teacher, who we mostly think of as enforcing silly rules and never laughing at all.

Mrs. W. have two other children, Darlene and Edgar, but Benny was the last one at home. He always been quiet, never have close friends, never have a girlfriend that I know of, though one time Pauline Cardinal had a real crush on him, toss herself right into his arms when we was riding in the back of Louis Coyote's pickup. Benny just peel her off him, like he was untangling himself from a thicket of weeds. He wasn't unfriendly, he just wanted it clear that he didn't want anybody too close to him.

The odd thing always been that while Mrs. W. encourage us to drop in any time because she like for Benny to have friends around, often when we were there Benny wasn't. Benny liked to go for long walks alone. Or he'd be with us for a while, then he'd go to his room, nobody would even notice him leaving, and while we'd be watching videos or just talking and joking around, Benny would be alone in his room playing Garth Brooks tapes and CDs. Still, nobody ever had a thought of his committing suicide until it happened.

We got a lot of suicide on the reserve, usually it have to do with drink or drugs. Bedelia and her social worker friends have their theories about why us Indians have a ten times higher suicide rate than everybody else, but it ain't something most of us even want to think about. My friends are just as queasy about suicide as me. We've all lost friends and several of us relatives, but it is like talk of suicides is behind one of them steel fire doors like they have at Blue Quills Hall. Nobody ever opens one of them steel reinforced doors.

Most of us attend the funeral, but we're shy and uncomfortable even shaking hands with Madelaine White Hand, and afterwards we can't get away fast enough, and even though we know we should, none of us stop by her house all the rest of this long winter.

When I suggest that the group of us should call on Mrs. White Hand on Mother's Day morning, spend the day keeping her company, and helping her out whatever way we can, for an answer I get mainly silence.

"I wouldn't know what to say," my girlfriend Sadie whisper to me, and is everybody else's attitude, too.

"We owe her," I argue. "She been like a mom to several of you, and good friend to the rest of us. It ain't fair for us to drop her because Benny's dead and we don't know what to say or how to act."

Nobody disagree with me, but nobody is enthusiastic either. Surprisingly, it is Frank, who never been known to be charitable, who decide the matter.

"Brother Frank will lead you my friends. Brother Frank will spread compassion like extra-crunchy peanut butter on fresh bread. Once we get there it will be just like old times."

"Oh, sure," somebody mumble. But at nine o'clock Mother's Day morning we all meet at the coffee shop in the curling rink, have coffee and donuts, head over to Mrs. W.'s.

I knock at the door. Frank is right behind me. The others wait at the truck. There is our girlfriends, Sadie and Connie, Bedelia Coyote, Eathen Firstrider and Julie Scar, Rufus Firstrider and Winnie Bear, Robert Coyote and a girl named Veronique, who he picked up at the York Hotel bar in Edmonton last night. Robert and Veronique just arrived, don't look like either of them had any sleep. Veronique is dressed in pink tights, a low cut blouse, a rose colored suede bomber jacket and the highest high heels I ever seen. I can only guess how Veronique usually spends her evenings.

"Once I told her what we was doing she says she got to come along. She thinks her own mom is probably dead, and she don't know where to look if she ain't," Robert whisper to me, while we waiting for his order of coffees to go. I think for maybe the first time in his life Robert Coyote, who is about the toughest dude on the reserve, is embarrassed. There's a big difference being seen with a girl like Veronique at midnight and being seen with her at nine in the morning.

Mrs. W. is a sight, in a long pink quilted housecoat, her hair going in ten directions at once, her flat, high-cheekboned face sleepy and vulnerable without her glasses.

"Happy Mother's Day," I say, and I hand her the present I bought, a video of *Tootsie*, which I know is one of her favorite movies, and was on sale at 7-Eleven for $4.95 when I buy a giant Slurpy.

"Never fear, Fencepost is here, offering sympathy, compassion, and for a small fee a clear conscience."

I figure that is about as gross a thing as someone could say to a mother lost her son about seven months ago, but

Madelaine White Hand unleash that laugh that is unique to her. "An explosion of goodwill," Bedelia Coyote calls it.

"Frank, I've really missed you," Mrs. W. says, give Frank a big hug. "None of your sweet talk works on me, remember I knew you when you were a cheap crook," and she laugh so loud the people at the truck start straggling up the sidewalk.

"Your laugh is still contagious, like pink eye," says Frank, who always make Mrs. W. laugh, usually by telling stories. I been playing straight man to Frank for so long, it's become natural for me to interrupt him at certain points, to tell the audience what really happened.

For instance, right after we get settled in Mrs. W.'s living room, she have the coffee on and we is handing out donuts from the box we bought at the cafe, Frank start to tell a story about one of the times he passed me and him off as expert hunting and fishing guides. This time we get dropped off from a helicopter in total wilderness, might be Alberta, British Columbia, or the North West Territories, at a spot where a lake run into a river, where the fishing supposed to be the best in the world.

"Lucky for us, the three fishermen we're guiding know how to pitch a camp, and they also know how to set up the collapsible boat been dropped off with us, and how to fish," Frank say, grinning happily. "Me and Silas here, we snared a few suckers in Jump Off Joe Creek, out back from Hobbema Pool Hall, but that pretty well summarize our fishing experience.

"I size up the river, walk along the bank, talk to the skies, the rocks, the bullrushes, pretend to hear voices from the earth tell me where the best places to fish are. I just act like I know what I'm doing, tell them where to cast their lines. It always amaze me how much people trust you if you just pretend you know what you're doing. For insurance, I have Silas make lots of sandwiches and keep their cups full of Jack Daniels."

"Silas, is this true?" ask Mrs. W., got one hand in front of her face, that laugh of hers revving up in her throat.

"Pretty much so far," I say, "you know Frank he could sell a plastic musk ox to a real Inuit soapstone carver."

"For once things go well and it look like we going to get away with our scam," Frank go on. "But then they want to fish the lake, so we all pile into their collapsible aluminium boat. They cast their lines and within a few minutes catch this huge fish, a northern pike, they say. I only recognize canned fish, like Red Salmon and Charlie the Tuna. This fish come leaping along the surface of the water like a jet ski, and it take the fishermen about twenty minutes to tire him out and haul him into the boat. Unfortunately, this fish was very alive, alert and angry, and the fisherman whose name was Duncan, got him by the tail and for whatever reason, look that fish right in the eye. Knowing my duty as a guide, and, as always, being oblivious to the dangers rampant in Mother Nature, I risked my own well being by stepping selflessly between man and fish."

At this point I interrupt.

"What actually happened was Frank, instead of keeping quiet and out of the way, pretended he knew something about fishing and decided to play guide. As soon as the fish came over the side of the boat, Frank took the line away from Mr. Duncan, managed to get the fish off the hook. Frank does step in where fools fear to tread; I don't even want to touch one of those big slimy fish."

The Firstrider brothers and Robert Coyote, who been fishing all their lives, jeer me.

"Frank get a grip with both hands on the tail of the fish, mumble a lot of gibberish that he tell the fishermen is an Indian prayer asking forgiveness of the fish for catching and killing him. The fishermen eat up this genuine Indian guide act, and Frank get so carried away he decide that the climax to his act will be to turn the fish around and kiss it on the nose."

Frank continue the story as if I ain't even spoken.

"I saved that rich American from goodness knows what. I shoved my face right in front of his, and while it may have looked to Silas that I was trying to kiss the fish, I was actually sacrificing my body to protect my client.

"My act of sacrifice resulted in me being at close range when that fish, while snapping at my client, accidentally bit me on the nose. Now, as we all know, a Fencepost is born with a high pain threshold. My uncle, Augustus Fencepost got pinned under a tree, miles from anywhere, when it was 40 below in the winter, and in order to survive had to amputate his right arm with his hunting knife, above the elbow. His only complaint was that he had to work with his left hand and he figure it took him twice as long to cut the right arm off as it would have the left. Uncle Augustus says he never passed out once 'cause he knew he'd die of frostbite and exposure if he did.

"But, I tell you, even after the first shock wore off I had a hard time remaining stoic, like my clients expected, not flinching or crying out while pretending that being bitten on the nose by a 20-pound pike is a regular occurrence for a Indian guide."

"What really happened," I say, after Frank stop to take a breath, "was Frank screeched so loud, after he kissed the fish and it hooked onto his nose, that birds rose up out of the trees on shore a quarter of a mile away. Frank danced around the boat, slapping at the fish attached to his nose and screaming. Mr. Duncan tried to step out of his way and fell overboard into the water that is icy even in July."

"It is not a guide's fault when a client cannot keep his cool in an emergency," says Frank, apparently unperturbed that I am making a liar out of him.

"The other two fishermen haul Mr. Duncan out of the water, head the boat back to shore where they can get him out of his wet clothes and in front of a fire. I am trying to calm Frank down, but he keep on yowling like a cat with its tail permanently closed in a door. I figure the sure way to free up his nose is to kill the fish. There is a big knife on the floor of the boat, so I lay Frank down on his side, place one of my boots on his head to keep him and the fish still, get a good grip on the fish's tail and decapitate that fish with more strokes of the knife than I would have hoped for.

"Unfortunately, even after the fish's body been detached from its head, the head remain locked on to Frank's nose. I guess that fish figure that as long as he's attached to Frank's nose he ain't gonna have to admit he's dead."

Here in Mrs. W.'s living room, ever since the part where the fish latched onto Frank's nose, Mrs. W. been guffawing and howling with laughter so wild and free and happy that everybody else joined in, until there is this group of people sitting around with tears spilling down their cheeks, all huffing and puffing like they just run a mile.

"Two of the fishermen taken off their jackets and wrapped them around Mr. Duncan. They look at Frank, still flat in the bottom of the boat, howling like a wolf with a stomach ache, the fish head clamped tight on his nose.

"'Jesus, Kid,'" one of them says to me, "'you gone and ruined our fish. We wanted to get some photographs. Can't hardly show off a photo of our fish's head attached to the nose of Leaping Lizard, or whatever he said his name was. I bet this is one big one he wishes had gotten away. If I didn't know better I'd swear he didn't know a thing about being a guide.'"

The odd thing is that no matter how many lies Frank get caught in, or how incompetent he proves himself, the victim always believes part of his story. In this case it was that Frank listed several organizations that he claimed he was a member, like Hunting and Fishing Guides of America, and International Association of Hunting Guides. He flash what he claim was membership cards, bright colored printing that do have his name in big letters, but was actually cut out from ads sent out from these Publishers Clearing House guys who promise that if you buy subscriptions to ten magazines no one ever heard of, Ed McMahon going to deliver ten million dollars to your door.

"Well," says Frank, "as usual Silas don't have the whole story. While I admit to being in a certain amount of pain I was, as always, more concerned with the welfare of my clients than myself. What Silas and my clients may have mistaken for cries of pain were actually genuine Indian prayers, mainly for the welfare of poor Mr. Duncan, who I was afraid would suffer exposure and hypothermia. And while I was somewhat disappointed that the fish didn't relinquish its grip when Silas chopped its head off, a mighty messy job of decapitation, I must say, I soon gathered my resources and kept on praying all through the flight back to civilization and up until the time a doctor was able to detach the fish from my nose."

Eventually the hunters have to radio for the helicopter, that probably wasn't even back to civilization yet, have it turn around and come get us. The hunters tell the pilot that they'll stay behind, that they don't need no guides anymore.

But the pilot tell them there is some federal regulations that they can't fish these waters unless they've got a guide with them, which was how they come to hire us anyway, no questions asked. He say is some kind of make-work legislation been passed so every rich hunter from outside Canada have to have a guide whether they need one or not.

That's just the way Canada is. One time I got interviewed by the CBC Television, a couple of guys worked while six more stood around and looked bored because their union said they had to.

"'In that case we'll keep the kid. What did you say your name was?'"

"I have to think fast, I think Frank introduce me as Nathan Timberwolf, but then it might have been Roscoe Smudgepot, Silas Threeballs or any of a dozen smooth-as-lies names roll off Frank's tongue.

"'I'm not licensed,' I say. 'Only my boss, Mr. Lizard, have all his Government papers.'"

"'Fucking bureaucracy,'" the fishermen say. But there's nothing they can do about it. All five of us and the gear and the collapsible boat, what still dripping water and wet weeds, get jammed into the helicopter, where we all have to listen to Frank scream for the whole flight back.

"Do they have any laws in Canada against mercy killing?" says Mr.Duncan, whose teeth is still chattering.

Frank is right, it is almost like old times. Eathen, Rufus and Robert rake the lawn, clip the caragana hedge, take off the storm windows, whitewash the rocks run on both sides of the sidewalk and form a flower bed in the center of the yard.

Me and the girls clean out Benny's room, get his clothes ready to go to the Goodwill in Wetaskiwin. Mrs. W. offer each of us some of his records and CDs, but all except Frank say no. I think Veronique is younger than any of us would of guessed. She follow Mrs. W. around like a shadow, tell her more than most of us would ever dream of, more than most people would want to listen to.

"My sister Gladys, Tiffany was her street name, she killed herself last winter about the same time as your boy," she tell Mrs. W. "She got picked up in the alley back of the International Hotel by three guys in a Jimmy. I took the license number, we do that for each other. An hour later they dropped her off on 104th Avenue by the York Hotel. I don't know what happened but Gladys walked off down 96th Street toward the river, disappear in the cold fog and exhaust. There was frost on all the electric wires and trees. People say she walked in a straight line out on the river until the ice gave way. They ain't found her body."

Mrs. W. give that girl a big hug.

And it ain't an hour later that she says to Veronique: "You know I sure get lonesome here, and I was thinking that if you needed a place to stay for a while . . . "

"My name's Ella," the girl say, tears oozing out of her eyes and trailing down her cheeks with her mascara.

I reduce my estimate of her age another two years.

"I got a pair of boots you could wear if you . . . " and again the girl interrupt by sighing and kicking off the spike heels, which Connie Bigcharles pick right up and when they fit she offer to trade a pair of jeans and a sweater for them.

After that the girls all take Ella into their group and it become obvious she ain't going back to Edmonton any time soon.

Mrs. W. hug us all goodbye and there is even a tear in her eye as she tell us how much it mean not to be alone on Mother's Day.

We didn't figure Ella to stay more than a few days, for some reason girls who been on the street usually get anxious for the excitement they left behind, but not Ella. She's been three months now with Mrs. W. and there's even some talk of her going into ninth grade when school starts in September.

"Sorry, Ma," I said when I finally got home about ten that evening, handing her a rose in a vase I bought at North Wind Florists in Wetaskiwin yesterday. The rose lived in Louis Coyote's pickup truck all this time, and after one of its thorns stick to the sleeve of Frank's jean jacket it got dragged out onto the asphalt in front of the pumps at Fred Crier's Texaco garage. The vase bounced a couple of times, spilled all its water and a couple of petals, suffer a chip on the rim and a crack at the base. We refilled the vase with the water hose at the gas station.

Ma give me an up and down look, like a woman used to receiving presents that are a day late and have suffered a certain amount of damage.

"I'm sorry," I say again, "I should have been here earlier, I ... "

"I know where you been," Ma said. She reached out and hugged me then, the rose, still clutched in her hand, scratched the back of my neck as her hands clasped together.

"I don't know what I done that you should have turned out so good," Ma says.

"I should have been here ... "

"I can have you any day of the year," she said. I just loaned you out to Madelaine White Hand for a few hours. You served double duty today."

The Secret
of the Northern Lights

For Evelyn Harper

t happened when I was just a girl," Etta our medicine lady says to me. We are sitting at Etta's kitchen table drinking Earl Grey tea, my favorite kind, and Etta's too. I just bought a box of one hundred bags in Edmonton this afternoon. I been asking Etta if she knows any scary stories I can retell to my kid sister, Delores and her friends, who like to gather round me in our cabin on nights when the wind is high and pine branches rub eerily against the window glass.

"Tell us a scary story," they say. Then they giggle and scream when I tell about ax murderers and ghosts and government officials.

"Dolphus Red Salmon was an Indian from further north than any of us, even my father, Buffalo-who-walks-like-a-man, ever been," says Etta. "Great Slave Lake was where he said he came from. Said the lake was so big you couldn't see from one side to the other, and it was so cold chunks of ice the size of boxcars floated around even in August.

"Dolphus Red Salmon had a starved and frazzled look about him, like someone who ain't had a good night's sleep in their life. His face was sharp and pointed like a fox, his black eyes dark and secretive. He was strong though, for a little man, his arms solid as cables. Used to swing me and my sister round and round, lift us right off our feet. And I never been of a delicate build even when I was only twelve years old.

"'I got this here secret, eh,' Dolphus Red Salmon said after he been around the reserve a few days. 'I know things that maybe I'm not supposed to.'

"'Yeah, sure,' people said, and went about their business.

"Dolphus Red Salmon arrive on the reserve carrying more stuff than it should be legal for one Indian to own. He step off the southbound Greyhound carrying a huge black suitcase with lots of straps and locks, that is about half as tall as he is. He drop it on the gravel, have to drag it up to the porch of Ben Stonebreaker's General Store because it too heavy to carry in a regular way. From the stomach of the bus the driver and Dolphus drag two more suitcases, a metal steamer trunk with a domed lid, and a canvas sack look like there could be a couple of logs trussed up inside.

"'Had to pay for that sack just like it was another passenger,' Dolphus say to us kids standing around staring at him, as the bus grumble off leaving purple fumes hanging in the air. 'And my trunk, too.'

"'What you got in there, Mister?' I ask. He is wearing denim overalls glazed with dirt, a red-and-black checkered mackinaw over a red western shirt with pearl buttons, and moccasins with red and yellow bead work that seen many a mile.

"'I'm lookin' for your medicine man.'

"'I can take you to him,' I say. 'He's the best medicine man in the world.'

"'So I hear. You wouldn't be his little girl, would you?'

"I notice he's got a pack of Vogue tobacco in the pocket of his mackinaw, along with a red packet of Chanticleer cigarette papers for building his roll-yer-owns.

"'You get one of your friends to guard my stuff and I'll give them a quarter.'

"'Give me the quarter and I'll guard your stuff. Anybody can take you to my father.'

"A kid named Amos Big Ears took him to meet my father. Buffalo-who-walks-like-a-man wasn't anything like his name, or like me. He was skinny and wiry, all angles, like five coat hangers tangled together.

"I must have sat for two hours in the sun in front of Ben Stonebreaker's store before I hear some harness bells. Funny, after all these years I can still hear those bells clear as yesterday. And when I hear them I expect our team of blacks to come ambling over the hill pulling my father's wagon. That day my father was all hunched over, the top of his tweed cap pointing ahead, his eyes on the wagon tongue. Dolphus Red Salmon sit beside him, smoking a cigarette.

"'I have big secrets,' Dolphus say.

"'So you say,' answers Papa.

"'I can create forces I don't understand.'

"'Like what?'

"'You wouldn't believe me. You'll have to see for yourself. I can have everything set up in three days if you'll help me. I already walked through the woods back there,' and he point to the west. 'There's a clearing back there where we can set everything up'

"'There's no need to be so mysterious,' says Papa. 'I have lived magic. I have conversed with spirits. I have met strange people who make wasteful claims . . . '

"Later on, at the table in our cabin, Dolphus was shovelling in pan-fried potato and venison steak with wild mushrooms like he hadn't eaten for days.

"'What I'm saying is you don't need to pretend with me' Papa said. 'If you're down on your luck and need a place to stay, you don't need to pretend to have a story. You're welcome here regardless.'

"'No. No.' Say Dolphus. 'You won't believe what I lug down here with me. You'll laugh.' He touch his temple. 'You'll say I been touched by the moon.'

"'What do you know what the rest of us don't?' I asked. Dolphus chewed for quite a while. Finally he swallow.

"'What I know,' he say to me and Buffalo-who-walks-like-a-man, 'is the secret of the Northern Lights.'

"They load all of Dolphus' suitcases and stuff into the wagon box and we head back toward our cabin. My father don't say nothing, but I guess that Dolphus Red Salmon impress him enough that he willing to study whatever is in that trunk and suitcases.

"Dolphus set up his equipment in a clearing maybe a hundred yards behind our cabins. To get there you had to walk through a dark grove of pine; there was no grass on the floor of the forest, just twigs and brown pine needles like a carpet. The clearing was the highest point of land for quite a ways. The grasses were dry for there hadn't been much rain that summer, a few asters, a tiger lily or two, and a few stalks of Indian paintbrush grew in the clearing.

"Papa's friend, Louis Six Shooter, a big, broad man walk like a bear, hardly ever say a word and was so strong I seen him pull saplings up by their roots, help them out. Louis is a gentle man, have a pretty young wife, and a daughter named Sue who I play with sometimes.

"First thing Dolphus did was build a log frame about 10′ x 6′, and six feet high. He and Louis Six Shooter peel the logs and in the July sun they dry white as ghosts.

"I wish I could tell you what all was there. I was only twelve and had never been anywhere, but I'd guess that if I saw Dolphus Red Salmon's set up today I still wouldn't recognize much of it. There were some circular brass discs, maybe six or eight, about eighteen inches across. There was copper tubing, not like what some men used to make moonshine, but thick coils of pipe close to two inches wide. There was a little boiler heated by a small cast iron stove, the kind used in winter to heat cattle-watering troughs. There were other things, too. Silver metal in shapes I never seen before or since, red and yellow and blue and green wires that joined all those shiny things together, and in one corner, an upside down glass sealer with a top the shape of a bald man's head.

"That glass was thick and bluey-green the color of telephone pole insulators that came along years later. And that glass jar, once the stuff got operating looked like it was full of lightning bugs.

"When everything set up, Dolphus unroll that bundle look like it could be full of logs, and cover the whole contraption with a whitish, gauze-like material I couldn't identify, but it was tough as fishing line and kept out rain and let in sunshine.

"'It draw from the sun in the day,' Dolphus said. 'Then at night it draw from the Northern Lights. I was told your father was the strongest medicine man anywhere, that's why I decide to share this with him. I need to learn what to do with what I know.'

"'Northern Lights shine brightest in winter,' I say. 'When the frost first scratch at your nose the Northern Lights come right out of the sky, surround you with green light that buzz like a blow fly, and is so real I swear I could touch it. Papa says there is something not exactly magic, but more sinister about the Northern Lights, and he sometimes wonder aloud about what kind of power they have.'

"'I know what kind of power they have,' say Dolphus. 'That's why I come here.'"

"Silas," Etta say to me. "I hear that in different parts of the world inventors work on the same things at the same time."

"I've read that," I say. "Somebody in Italy and somebody in Australia splitting the same atom, or grafting the same kind of polkadot rose."

"Well, Papa and Dolphus were on the same wavelength, and they found each other at the right time, for it was Papa's idea that put the machine into full action."

"'By God, I never thought of that,' Dolphus say to Papa. 'That is gonna make it work. I knew there was a reason I come here.'

"I never did know what suggestion it was that Papa made.

"A few people come to stare but the whole apparatus sit silent as an abandoned car covered in cheesecloth. At night there is nobody around except Papa, Dolphus and me. It is at night, at least on clear nights that the machine begin to come alive.

"When the summer sky finally get dark, the Northern Lights come creeping up the sky, sluicing around like silk scarves, humming the way power lines do nowadays.

"Maybe a week after Papa and Dolphus get everything set up, I wake with a start in the middle of the night, moonlight like a white blanket across my bed and the floor of the room. I pick up the old Wesclox that sits on the floor by the bed, hold it into the moonlight. It is three in the morning. What I hear is this humming, like a thousand humming birds, a million bees. It is like the air is full of sounds that could be touched. I wave my hands as if I could catch handfuls of sound.

"I was sleeping in a T-shirt. I pull on jeans and moccasins and head out toward the sound. It surrounds me, makes my head feel light, achy. I scrunch my eyes to get away from it but I can't.

"I find Papa and Dolphus sitting on a log at the edge of the clearing, smoking, watching the machine. Dolphus had been talking but he stop when he see me.

"'It's alright. You can talk in front of Etta,' Papa say. 'I'm going to teach her everything. I've already started.'

"'A woman?' says Dolphus, his voice skeptical.

"'She has the gift,' Papa say.

"I didn't understand what he meant then. It was a lot of years later before I understood.

"The first time I seen it I thought it was funny. 'Look at that, Papa,' I said, and giggled like crazy. Papa was drinking tea at the kitchen table. Dolphus was asleep in his blanket on the floor.

"Outside in the yard one of the fat Rhode Island Red hens, with its orange eyes and blood-colored comb was scratching around in the chickweed. The sun was already hot, the dew mostly off the grass. What I was laughing at was that the big red hen was casting a shadow, not hen-shaped, but short and stick-like, the shadow of a prairie dog standing on its hind legs.

"I had to ask Papa three times before he looked. I guess Papa had been up until dawn, out with Dolphus by the machine in the clearing.

"Papa didn't laugh. He studied the hen for a while. He sipped his tea.

"'Take a walk around, Etta. See if there's anything else going on.'

"Papa started some water to boil on the wood stove, and stood studying his roots and herbs that were tied in bunches, hanging all along the wall next to the stove.

"When I stepped outside I screamed. I had the shadow of a pony. A small, shaggy pony, a Shetland, one like Winston Dodginghorse owned.

"'Papa!' I yelled.

"He stood in the doorway of the cabin, staring. I moved cautiously around the yard, but whether my shadow was in front or behind me, it remained a pony.

"'Dolphus! Get up!' Papa yelled.

"It wasn't until then that it occurred to me that what was happening might have something to do with Dolphus' machine.

"'Dolphus! Get out here!' my father cried again.

"Dolphus appeared in the doorway buttoning his plaid shirt. His hair was wild and spiky, his eyes surprised by the sunlight.

"'What?'

"My father pointed. Dolphus' eyes became alert, but wary as a bird's. He reached automatically for the Vogue tobacco and cigarette papers in his shirt pocket.

"'You stay here, Etta,' Papa said. 'Go inside and make your shadow disappear.' He took Dolphus' arm and led him in the direction of the grove of trees and the machine. Papa's shadow was his own, but Dolphus' was of a hunch-shouldered hawk sitting on a limb, ready to launch itself toward something unfortunate.

"I went inside and started cooking up a breakfast of flapjacks and fat back. Once, I went to the screen door and held my arms out and saw a shadow of my arms and hands. I wondered if the pony was still behind me, but not enough to step out into the sun and test it.

"It was hardly an hour later when the first people showed up looking for Papa, hoping for treatment. An old man with the shadow of a shovel, a woman followed by three tall hollyhocks, a big farmer named Stockton Quail with a clenched fist for a shadow."

"I wish Frank Fencepost was here to hear this story," I say to Etta. "You know what Frank would want for a shadow?"

"I can imagine," says Etta.

"A scary thing that I remember was that your papa, Paul Ermineskin, though he was just a toddler, maybe three years old, have a shadow twice or more as big as him, a snarling, fanged black beast like nothing me or my Papa ever seen before.

"'Go home and close your doors. See what tomorrow brings,' he told everyone, which worried me, since that meant Papa didn't have a clue what was going on.

"One old woman, whose shadow was a swooping owl, ran keening into Jump Off Joe Creek. Her grandchildren had to pull her out, and even though it was July, build a fire in the space heater to dry her clothes.

"The next morning it was cool and cloudy with a driving rain that eventually lasted two days. When the sun reappeared on the third morning everyone had their own shadows again, and no matter how they danced, or ran, or circled on the street in front of Ben Stonebreaker's Store, they had only shadows in their own image.

"Papa was solemn-faced for those three days. Him and Dolphus whisper some, but mainly Papa sit with his tea cup in his hand, thinking, his eyes open but far, far away.

"'Why?' I ask Papa that first evening, after I cook up some prairie chicken he shot back in the meadow, bread it good in flour and sprinkle lots of salt and pepper.

"'I don't know, daughter,' he says.

"'Do you think it has to do with?' and I nod toward Dolphus sit on the log steps of our cabin smoking a roll-yer-own.

"'I think so. He says he heard voices out of the sky tell him to build that there machine. He claim this business with the shadows has happened before, way up north where he live. People who hear voices that tell them to do things are usually touched by the moon. But Dolphus is different. Far as I can tell he's smart and serious, and scared to death by what he's created out there.'

"'Why is he scared? The business with the shadows is harmless.'

"'He says other things have happened.'

"'Like what?'

"'He doesn't say. But he's afraid, and that makes me afraid.'

"'Why not take the machine apart?'

"'Because we are living at an extraordinary moment. We are about to experience things no man has ever seen. What I want to determine is if anything good can come from this machine. This business with the shadows make it look like a trickster is at work. But what if it could cure the lung disease or make the heart beat longer, or the eyes see better.

I have to know what it's capable of doing, both good and bad.'

"'Why do you think it didn't reveal itself to a medicine man first, instead of Dolphus Red Salmon?'

"But Papa didn't answer. His eyes went far away as he tried to see into the future, and his tea got colder and colder.

"Papa and Dolphus spend every clear night in the meadow with the machine.

"I go out there sometimes while the Northern Lights are brewing in the clear, starry sky. It seem like their center, their core, is right above us, and they raining sheets of green silk down on us. It is light as day and the air thick with electricity. There are stories of men turning into wolves on this kind of night.

"The machine, under its white cover, rumble and gurgle like a full stomach, make some other noises as if there were wild animals inside, straining to get out.

"I was the first one it happened to. A full day before anybody else. I dreamed this odd dream. I was a cat, and I was pussy-footing through damp grass just high enough to tickle my belly. I poked my way through some taller grass, nose first, ears back, face pointed as a spear. My hearing was acute, but it was as if I was walking on foot-thick moss, I made no sound at all.

"As I pushed through the tall grass I froze, my senses electric. In front of me was a puddle of water and in it a sparrow was bathing, flopping about, making cheep-cheep sounds, not thinking of danger. Beside the puddle were two more sparrows, each busy drinking, bending forward taking on water, tipping back their heads to swallow. The one washing was a sure thing.

"I became a coiled spring, flattening myself to the earth, silently digging a foothold with my back claws. I sprang and hit the unsuspecting sparrow full force, had his neck in my teeth before he knew what happened. There was a screech and a whirr as the other two took flight. I salivated. The smell of blood and terror was overwhelming."

"Wow!" I said. "Is that when you woke up?"

"I woke up at the same time as my old mottled cat, Minneaux, who was sleeping in the crook of my arm. The cat and I exchanged the strangest glance. I knew without a doubt that I had been having the cat's dream.

"I told Papa of the dream at breakfast and he laughed the way a kindly father laughs at a foolish child.

"'I'll bet the cat was having your dream,' Papa said. 'I bet she was dreaming of that skinny boy, Lawrence Black Horses, who brings you partridges and wild flowers.'

"'Oh, Papa,' I said, embarrassed.

"'Bet the cat wondered what it was doing kissing that skinny boy.'

"But I knew what had happened, and when I caught Dolphus Red Salmon's eye he ducked his head to his flapjacks, but not before I saw the fear, like a sneaky animal, in his eyes.

"The next night I slept well, but in the morning when Lawrence Black Horses came by, shy as a fawn, with a few tiger lilies in a Aylmer's tomato can with its dark green label, he told me about his dream. He was rich, a storekeeper trying to decide how many cases of Kellogg's Cornflakes to order, how many mops and how many galvanized buckets. And he was counting money and keeping books.

"'Simon Stonebreaker,' I said.

"'Who?'

"'You had Simon Stonebreaker's dream.'

"'That's silly,' said Lawrence.

"'Simon Stonebreaker is a storekeeper, trader, fur buyer. You ever do anything like that?'

"'I sell him muskrat pelts, collect bounty for magpie legs.'

"'What do you reckon Simon Stonebreaker dreams of?'

"I told him about me and the cat.

"'That's even sillier,' he said. 'I wish I hadn't told you.'

"By the end of the day Lawrence Black Horses find out he ain't alone. People come in a steady stream to see Papa, saying they've had weird or scary dreams or just the kind of dreams they've never had before and they want Papa to interpret what's happened to them. I notice that most of those who come by are the same ones who had their shadows fouled up. They are also the people who have been back to the clearing to stare at the machine.

"At supper that night Papa ask Dolphus, 'Has this happened before?'

"'What?' say Dolphus evasively.

"'The dreams. People who seen your contraption having strange dreams, maybe other people's dreams?'

"'Nooooo,' say Dolphus after a long pause, dragging the word out way too long.

"'You better tell me if you know something you ain't told me,' Papa say. 'We workin' on dangerous ground here. Nothin' good can come from this kind of business.'

"'There was a couple of things,' Dolphus say.

"'Like what?'

"'I had the dreams of a tree.'

"'A tree? How could you know?'

"'I knew. Trees dream of lightning, of caterpillars, of double-bitted axes. Frightening dreams. You ever dream you're afraid of being chopped down, peeled, your limbs lopped off and you're turned into a corral pole?'

"'No.'

"'I did. It was the dream of a tree grew behind my cabin up north. And the really weird part was I had thought of turning that tree into a corral pole.'

"'Other people?' ask Papa.

"'My wife, she had the dreams of a fire-eyed steer we were fattening up for winter. She don't understand. She won't let him be killed. She lives in terror. I brought everything to you. You're said to have a certain power.'

"'How did this business come to you?'

"'I was ice fishing. Sitting under a canvas by a hole in the lake, burning a lantern to keep away loneliness, when the Northern Lights spoke.'

"'What did they say?' ask Buffalo-who-walks-like-a-man.

"'They tell me to gather and build, and I do as they say.'

"'And?'

"'Nothing more.'

"Papa sit silent for a long time nursing his tea.

"It was that fellow Louis Six Shooter who change quite a few lives forever. Louis grew a red willow clump for a shadow and it amuse him. He smile slow as he lumber about our yard showing it off.

"'Your old red hen can hide her chicks in my shadow,' Louis Six Shooter say to me, and he smile long and slow, enjoying his joke.

"But it is not funny when Louis return to our yard, moving fast for him, anxious to see Papa, the day after people begin having strange dreams.

"There are tears leaking out of his eyes when I answer his tap on the door. He cough and sniffle and start right in to tell Papa about his dream.

"'Go outside, Etta,' Papa say to me, and I can tell by his serious face that I shouldn't argue or ask any questions.

"Papa and Louis Six Shooter stay in the cabin for a couple of hours, while so many people come that they form a line outside, people who have had each other's dreams, the dreams of animals or rocks, or flowers. Imogene Binder even have a white man's dream.

"Louis Six Shooter look heartbroken when he finally come out of the cabin. I walk with him down the hill toward Simon Stonebreaker's store.

"'Can I help?'

"'I can't tell you, Etta. It's too awful for a little girl to hear.'

"But it ain't too awful for Papa to tell me late that night. He tell me because he was puzzled, because he can't figure out how to help Louis Six Shooter.

"'Louis is having his wife's dreams,' Papa said. 'His wife's dreams are clear and hot as fire. She dreams of a man named Dennis Ear, who is a cowboy, tough and handsome and has girls buzzing around him like he was honey.'

"'But are the dreams true?' I asked. 'Just because you dream something don't mean that it's happened or even that it going to happen?'

"'Not usually. But Louis Six Shooter been asking around, which mean he twisted an arm or two. Friends who been protecting him let him know that while he is away Dennis Ear been at his cabin, a lot.'

"'Are we really having dreams that belong to somebody or something else?'

"'Though I never seen anything like it, that's what it look like. It's another story now for Louis Six Shooter. He's confirmed in real life, what he learned from what he believes was his wife's dream.'

"The next day I see Louis sitting on the hitching post rail in front of Simon Stonebreaker's store. I never seen anyone looking so sad; he is slumped forward like his shoulders been turned to jelly.

"When he see me, he beckon me over, reach in his back pocket take out seven dollars and give it to me, a five and two ones.

"'Ain't gonna need it no more,' he said.

"That night me and Papa wake to the blast of a shot gun, both barrels, one after the other. When we run to the clearing we find Dolphus Red Salmon dead in his bedroll, with Louis Six Shooter slumped over him, his heart blown away.

"The RCMP from Wetaskiwin come around the next day, say it was a simple murder-suicide. Double murder, actually, for before he come to our place, Louis hit his wife with one of his huge hands, break her neck like kindling.

"The RCMP don't understand why, if it was Dennis Ear Mrs. Six Shooter was fooling around with, that Dolphus Red Salmon get killed. Dennis Ear, we hear later, got wind of Louis

Six Shooter's anger, and took off quick for a rodeo in Southern Alberta.

"Papa act solemn with the RCMP, two young officers, fresh scrubbed as Mormon Missionaries, who don't speak a word of Cree between them. Papa touch his heart, look sad, touch his head, let them know Louis Six Shooter was crazy with jealousy and grief, and that there was no reason for him to kill Dolphus Red Salmon. The RCMP trust papa, take his word for what happen.

"Papa loaded up everything from the clearing in our wagon box. I thought we was going to drive out in the wilderness west of the reserve and dump it in some secret spot, or I knew of a big lake a day or two's wagon ride west and north. I decided it must be that lake, after I seen Papa and Jerome Fencepost, your friend Frank's grandfather, hoist up a rowboat and lay it upside down over the wagon box. I suspect we gonna be gone more than two days when Papa have me pack hundred pound sacks of flour and oatmeal, with lots of tea, sugar, and smoked venison.

"'We're going to the place Dolphus come from,' Papa finally say, after I ask and ask.

"'Why so far?'

"'The world shrinks,' Papa said. 'There's no place safe to hide things around here. Too many people. Too many hunters in the woods, too many boats on the lakes. Eyes everywhere.'

"It took us over a month to make the trip. I still don't know how Papa knew the way. He just did. I didn't question him. We drove in the grassy ditches beside the roads, stopping often to let the horses rest, graze, drink. Some nights we slept in the wagon box, under the overturned boat. If the weather was warm, Papa spread a moosehide robe in a sheltered spot, and we slept side by side, each covered by our own blanket.

"Sometimes we'd stop in someone's farmyard, water our horses, maybe be invited in for a meal, but usually a couple of plates brought out to us. I think Papa could smell a reserve; when we found one we'd stop an extra day, rest the horses, repair the wagon or harness.

"North of Edmonton, the roads went from two-lane pavement, to gravel, to oiled dirt, to plain dirt, to grassy trails with wheel tracks and oil-slicked grass in between. Once, we crossed a valley that was wide and open and there were flowers swaying in the wind, blue, yellow, pink, far as I could see. We crossed rivers and creeks, some stone-bedded and shallow, one dark as ditchwater with whirlpools like eyes. If we hadn't had all of Dolphus' equipment on board we would have been swept away.

"It was a cold, rainy morning, the wind fresh as a slap, when we reached the little town Dolphus claimed to have come from. There were six houses all low and built from chinked logs, and a frame store with a log addition at the back that had once been painted white. Most of the paint was flaked off, but the word STORE in red paint that had turned pink with age, stood out on the false front.

"Papa went inside and was gone a long time. I slipped down to the floor of the wagon box, out of the wind, and pulled my brown slicker tight around me.

"'I don't reckon anyone cared enough to let Dolphus' wife know what happened,' Papa said several times during the long drive. 'That's what we'll do first. All this stuff is hers. Only right she should get to make the call on it.'

"The street in front of the store was all mud and water. Papa scrape his boots on the wagon wheel, climb onto the seat and take the reins.

"'They live a long ways off,' was all he said.

"We drove until mid-afternoon. The sky cleared, the sun gave off heat, but the wind was still brisk. Finally we came to a clearing where a low-slung log cabin lay. It had a slant roof, tin covered with sod, I guessed. Pigweed grew three feet high on the roof, ripe and bursting with its warty coils of seed. It looked like the door opened right into the side of a hill. There was a scrawny brindle steer behind the wooden fence of the corral. A red hen pecked in the dust in front of the cabin.

"Papa sat waiting until the door opened maybe six inches, but no one showed themselves. I knew we were at the right place, though. The yard was crammed with rusted farm machinery, ghost-gray pieces of threshing machines, discs, harrows, a plow or two that would never turn another furrow. There was a very old tractor dripping rust, its smokestack tipped to one side like a lightning-struck limb. There were boilers and galvanized tubs with rusted out bottoms, everything half hidden by August grass and weeds.

"Papa got down off the wagon, motioned for me to follow.

"He walked slowly to the door. He knocked gently, tap, tap. From inside I heard a baby cry, a dry, whimpering sound. I thought I could hear a dog snuffling, a growl on its tongue waiting to be loosed. I caught a whiff of sour air. I thought I heard a gun cocking.

"The door opened another six inches and the face of a thin, terrified woman appeared. Beside and behind her, some hanging on to her, some gripping the weather-stripped doorframe, were several small children. I counted four sets of brown, dirty fingers.

"Papa spoke gently to the woman, asking if this was Dolphus Red Salmon's place. She understood the name, and looking over our shoulders her black eyes appraised the loaded wagon. She did not understand anything else Papa said. These were, I think, Dog Rib Indians, or maybe not, but they didn't speak Cree and we didn't speak any other dialect.

"'What do you want?' the woman said slowly, in broke-up English, as if she was repeating a phrase she had memorized a long time ago.

"Papa looked at me. His English was limited to a few words.

"'Are you Dolphus Red Salmon's wife?' I asked, speaking slowly.

"She nodded.

"From behind her in the dank cabin I could smell the odors of sorrow.

"I couldn't bring myself to tell her the bad news. I let Papa tell her in Cree, then I translated to English. I seemed less responsible that way.

"She stared at us, her eyes full of at least suspicion if not anger.

"'He was,' she said, and not able to find the word in English, tapped her head and lifted her eyes toward the sky, where a white, icy slice of moon hung in the late afternoon sky.

"She indicated she wanted no part of the equipment we carried.

"'Spirits of night talked to him,' she said.

"I expected her to elaborate but she remained silent.

"'Are you alright?' I asked.

"She shrugged.

"'Do you have enough food?' I asked, prompted by Papa.

"From the darkness behind her a baby mewled again, a dry, sick sound.

"'I'm sorry,' I said, as Papa took my arm and led me back to the wagon.

"We unloaded what supplies we had left. We kept one 20 lb sack of oatmeal. We piled the supplies on the ground. When I started to carry a heavy sack of sugar toward the door, Papa held me back.

"'Leave her what pride she has,' he said in Cree. If I hadn't before, I understood then what a great man he was.

"That night we camped on the shore of the biggest lake I'd ever seen. No matter how I stared there was no other side to it. The water was cold as death.

"I helped Papa push the boat into the shallow water tangled with bull rushes and lily pads. The boat was dry from the long trip and water jumped through the cracks, as if the boat were thirsty, greedy for water.

"Back home Papa owned a birch bark canoe, and I trusted it, and I trusted Papa in it. I knew too that there was no room in it for Dolphus' equipment, which was why we'd traveled all this way with the rowboat.

"'A day or two,' Papa said, and he was right. The boat quenched its thirst, as it absorbed water the cracks closed. Those that continued to leak, Papa staunched with willow slivers.

"That night a V of geese crossed the lake heading south. The wind was bitter. The leaves were turning.

"'Will it snow?'

"'No,' Papa said. 'Good weather will last past the Goose Moon. We will be home before winter.'

"On the third afternoon we loaded all of Dolphus Red Salmon's boxes and equipment into the boat. By the time Papa and I got in the gray water was lapping at the top edges.

"Papa poled us out through the reeds into the bruise-colored water. The sun was high and the lake calm. Papa rowed slowly and steadily, and the shore receded until it was like a single long pencil line on paper.

"Darkness fell and still Papa rowed on. The moon rose and the Northern Lights came trotting up the sky like a wolf pack. That far north they had a life of their own. One time, Silas, you showed me a picture of a peacock's fanned out tail feathers. That was what the sky was like, all peacock tails and silk scarves.

"And they spoke. At first it was just their usual hum and buzz, like a field of beehives, but soon the sound became a language, and as I came to understand some of it, I stood up and stared into the roiling sky.

"'Don't listen,' Papa said, slowing the boat. 'Don't listen to what they have to say.'

"'Who are they, Papa?'

"'Better not to know.'

"Papa took one of the canvas-wrapped bundles and slipped it quietly overboard. He could have tossed it but he didn't. He deposited it as if he was feeding it to the lake.

"The Northern Lights flashed and boiled.

"'Stop him! Stop him!' they said to me.

"'Don't listen,' said Papa, easing one of the suitcases into the dark water.

"'We will tell you secrets,' they said to me, 'of shadows, dreams, desires. Whatever you want most will be yours.'

"'Don't listen,' Papa said again, handing the many-buckled suitcase to the lake.

"'I won't,' I said to Buffalo-who-walks-like-a-man. But, oh, I wondered what I might do if I were alone among those swirling lights, my heart's desire within my grasp. I felt great sorrow for Dolphus Red Salmon.

"Piece by piece, Papa sunk the metal working of Dolphus' contraption. The boat eased higher out of the water as each parcel dropped.

"A white linen moon hung to the left of us. Everything smelled of wind and water. The voices became fainter, their strength faltering as Papa continued to defy their wishes.

"We started back. The water was calm as blue velvet. The stars reflected in the lake looked like bright bobbing marbles.

"Buffalo-who-walks-like-a-man patted my hand, then went back to rowing. I stared up, I looked down. It was hard to tell if we were in the sky or on the lake."

PRINTED AND BOUND
IN BOUCHERVILLE, QUÉBEC, CANADA
BY MARC VEILLEUX IMPRIMEUR INC.
IN JULY, 1998